Dear Harlequin Subscriber,

The White Wave is sent to you as a
Free Bonus Gift. It is Harlequin's
way of saying thank you for your
continued patronage.
From the early days of Harlequin,
our primary objective has been to
bring you romance reading of the
highest quality.

Thank you,
Harlequin Reader Service

It was the loveliest ring she'd ever seen!

"It suits you, Guinevere," Adam said, as he slipped it on her finger. Jenny tore her eyes away from the ring to look up at him in bewilderment. This wasn't a present a man gave to a friend, she thought wildly, hopefully.

"Adam, it's beautiful," she stammered, "but you needn't have.... It must have been very expensive...."

She trailed off because on his face was the hard mocking expression she knew so well but had rarely seen the past couple of weeks.

"Oh, don't worry, Jennifer, it's to be expected of your eager fiancé. And what's a little money when everyone knows it paves the way to a woman's heart?" And with that he walked away, hands in his pockets, leaving her frozen in her chair by the warm fire.

The White Wave

Jocelyn Griffin

Harlequin Books

TORONTO • NEW YORK • LONDON
AMSTERDAM • PARIS • SYDNEY • HAMBURG
STOCKHOLM • ATHENS • TOKYO • MILAN

ISBN 0-373-2543-2

Published April 1983

CHAPTER ONE

PUSHING HER HAIR out of her eyes, Jenny sat back and surveyed her handiwork. The garden her mother had so loved bloomed riotously—and now weedlessly—around her, and the old gray stone house stood dozing quietly in the warm spring sun, up to its sills in glorious color. The tranquillity was, in a way, reassuring, but at the same time the sight of so much that had not changed served to remind Jenny of all that *had* changed.

Lying awake for long hours the previous night, she had decided to look for work in London and leave everything that was a tangible link to her parents. Some detached area of common sense knew that the decision was wise, but nevertheless the snapping of each fragile tie would hurt. Just once before had she left Cornwall for any length of time; even then she'd only gone to Devon to take a six-month secretarial course and had come home most weekends.

Ever since the day she'd returned home for good, with a certificate declaring she'd completed the course with honors, she had typed her father's manuscripts. In fact, after the first few weeks she'd shown such a grasp of the material that he asked her to edit when necessary. She did so expertly, and when he complimented her she grinned and said, "Chickens coming home to roost."

He was a historian, author of a number of scholarly books, and from earliest childhood her bedtime stories were always historical. By the time she was seven she could repeat in heartrending detail the fates of all six wives of King Henry VIII.

Her father had hoped his only child would choose to study history at university, and she was certainly qualified to do so. She had nearly made up her mind to apply when, walking suddenly into the kitchen one afternoon, she found her mother hunched over the sink, her face bluish and her breath coming in gasps. What followed decided Jenny on a secretarial college where she could finish the course quickly and be near home at the same time.

Shocked at her mother's condition, Jenny had made her sit down and, when the older woman's breath come more easily, demanded an explanation. The trouble, said her mother, was her heart, damaged by a childhood bout with rheumatic fever.

"Does Da know?" Jenny still called her father by this babyish name, begun years ago as a joke. She used it now unconsciously, joking never further from her mind.

"No. I couldn't bear to worry him unnecessarily."

"Unnecessarily?" Jenny squeaked.

"Yes, love, unnecessarily," her mother returned firmly. "It's unnecessary that he be worried by something that can't be altered one way or the other. When he first brought me here as a bride, I asked Neil Pennington about it, because I'd begun to wonder whether I ought to have told your father before we married. Neil was newly qualified and full of all sorts of technical language, but what he said confirmed my feeling that there was no reason to distress your father. He advised me to take reasonably good care of myself. I've done so, and we have never discussed it since."

Jenny was still disturbed, but her mother, color back in her face, said briskly, "Enough sober talk for one day; I'm fine now. Here, take your father's tea into the study and try to drag him from that welter of papers long enough to eat. I'll be right in with the sandwiches."

Tea had been a happy meal, her mother laughing and

teasing as usual, perfect foil to Jenny's quietly serious father. Convincing him that she'd prefer to read history at home as his typist, Jenny had attended the secretarial college but otherwise let her fears for her mother sink to the bottom of her mind. Eighteen months after Jenny finished college, her mother died quietly in her sleep.

Though neither of them knew how, Jenny and her father carried on. Without much trouble she added housework and cooking to her secretarial duties. In fact, she almost welcomed the extra jobs because they helped ease her grief.

If Jenny adjusted reasonably well, her father was another matter. Always the quiet one of the family, he became quieter. He was as affectionate as ever to his daughter, but she often saw on his face a look of complete stillness that troubled her. Remembering the sense of perfect harmony between her parents, she knew she could do nothing about that look.

At any rate, her father continued to work on his latest book, the subject being the minor saints of Britain, which he had been researching off and on for as long as she could remember. All she could do was hope that he'd be able to lose himself in his work and find some comfort that way.

The book was excellent, Jenny realized, as she edited and typed each chapter. Her father's work had always been scholarly, but this time his writing had a power and smoothness that made it more readable than ever before. Each chapter, after Jenny gave it its final polishing, was sent off to David Standish, her father's longtime friend and publisher.

The writing had been going so well that her father refused to stop even when he developed a case of flu; to Jenny's protests he responded that he wanted to finish the last chapter, then he'd relax. He *had* finished the last chapter and gone meekly to bed, where he lay quietly for two days, not getting any better. Late one afternoon, Jenny, who had been reading on the far side of the room, became conscious of a feeling of suspended motion and knew, sorrow clutching at her heart, that she was alone. Her father had died.

Neighbors took over—those kindly people who rally around in times of crises. For two weeks their unobtrusive help and quiet presence shielded Jenny from both solitude and responsibility. Numbly she accepted their assistance until her sense of shock began to fade.

She might have gone on drifting mindlessly where it not for Dr. Pennington. One evening, after work, he dropped by to sit in her mother's cheerful kitchen and drink the coffee Jenny listlessly brewed for him. Over the rim of his cup he looked at his friends' daughter with kindly eyes; then he began to speak in a tone that was deliberately brisk.

"Well, my dear, it's time you made some plans."

She looked at him apathetically, but he went on. "Because you're legally of age, you have no need of a guardian, but about a month ago your father asked me to be a sort of informal adviser to you if you ever needed one. As the doctor who delivered you and ministered to all your childhood aches and pains, I felt I already had a proprietary interest in you, so I agreed."

Knowing he wanted her to, Jenny managed to respond to his light remarks with a small, fleeting smile, but she said nothing.

"Do you know where you stand financially?"

This time she collected herself and answered. "Yes, I do. The lawyer explained things to me after the funeral." Her voice broke slightly on the last word, but she steadied it and continued. "By the terms of the will he made after mother died, the house and land are mine, along with a savings account and all further royalties from Da's work."

"That sounds, Jenny, as though with careful management

you could stay here and live as something of a lady of leisure. On the other hand, I certainly wouldn't advise it.''

Putting down his cup, he rose to his feet and walked to the other side of the warm, low-ceilinged kitchen, a room that still seemed filled with her mother's personality. Then he said abruptly, ''I think you should look for a job in London.''

''A job in London?'' Jenny repeated, startled out of her apathy.

''Yes, Jenny, just that.''

He strode back across the room and took both her hands in his, willing her to concentrate.

''Think for a moment. You're a trained secretary with more than two years' experience working for your father, editing as well as typing his manuscripts, and he was not an easy taskmaster, much as he loved you. His standards were high and you met them. Of course, you'd have to adjust to a new employer, but I'm convinced you could do it.''

He paused to check her expression; it was dubious, so he continued. ''I'm also convinced that you *should* do it, dear. Work is one of the best remedies for sorrow I can prescribe, and although you could get a job in this area and live here at home, I think a new place would be better for you. Getting to know it would take time and attention, and carry its own excitement as well.''

He released her hands, and Jenny stood up and walked to the window. Able to see little in the twilight beyond it, she turned back to the bright room.

''But what would I do with the house? I don't want to sell it!'' The last words tumbled out in a rush.

''Nor would you have to,'' he reassured her. ''If you rented the house, you'd have a bit more income, someone to keep an eye on things here and a chance to preserve your roots.''

She looked at him thoughtfully, and he was glad to see that

she was responding and beginning to be more herself. He was, however, both too wise and too fond of her to force her into making decisions yet.

"I won't push you, Jenny. I promised your father I'd give you the best advice I could, but you're a grown woman and not required to listen to my telling you what to do. And now I'll be on my way and let you get some sleep. Mind that you do, my girl!"

She smiled a little at the order that followed his disclaimer about telling her what to do, but nodded obediently. Shrugging into the familiar coat that seemed to be nearly as old as he was, he gave her a final wave and was gone. Alone in the quiet house, Jenny shut the door slowly behind him, then tidied up and prepared for bed. It was a long time, however, before she followed her old friend's order.

STANDING UP, Jenny swept together the limp weeds she had pulled from among her mother's flowers and dumped them into the compost heap. She brushed bits of earth and grass off her old canvas skirt and gave the garden a last, thoughtful look; then she walked quickly into the kitchen and picked up from the table the letters she'd typed early that morning.

She caught Dr. Pennington at the end of his morning office hours; he studied her for a moment as she stood at the door, then smiled and said, "Welcome back."

Jenny knew he wasn't referring to her appearance at his office. Coming in, she sat by his desk and handed him the papers she had been carrying. "For your approval."

The first was a letter to one of the larger secretarial agencies in London. He glanced at it and his eyes twinkled at her. "What? My quarrelsome Jenny agreeing with me?"

She picked up the reference to their years of uproarious arguments, when he had egged her on to disagree with him purely for the fun of it, and fired back, "The ugly truth is that in all our arguments I seem to wind up agreeing with you in the end. It does get to be habit forming.''

He chuckled and turned to the next item in her sheaf of papers, reading it with more attention. It was a letter to David Standish, informing him of her father's death. In it Jenny also explained that she hoped to be taking a job in London and would bring with her to his offices the finished final chapter of Owen Tremayne's last book.

It was a short letter, and when he had finished reading it the doctor looked up to see Jenny regarding the far wall of his office rather fixedly. He wisely said nothing and bent his head to the last item. It was a letter to the newspaper, inserting an advertisement of a furnished house to let. He read it, then put it on top of the others, neatly aligning their edges. Looking at her speculatively, he said, "I think I could save you a stamp."

Puzzled, she asked, "A stamp? Which one?"

"The one on the letter to the newspaper. I have a likely tenant for you if you're interested."

On that last sentence he stopped looking at her, and Jenny struggled momentarily with a mixture of irritation and amusement. He apparently knew quite well that agreeing with him in the end was a habit of hers, and he'd probably had a tenant in mind before she'd even known she'd wanted one.

Amusement predominated, and she made a small sound that was part snort, part laugh, while he met her eyes with a grin of acknowledgment.

"Who is it?" she asked.

"Old Mrs. Graham's nephew, Blair. I've been in and out over there lately, checking on her arthritis, and yesterday I found the two of them in the middle of an argument. He's been down here for a week or so, on a painting holiday from London, and would like to stay on. But he doesn't want his aunt to have the trouble of looking after him. She insists he's no trouble, but he'd still like to rent a house in the village so that he can stay here to paint and visit his aunt often without being a nuisance to her.''

''I see.''

Her voice was suddenly flat, and she stared down at her small hands, which clasped each other tightly. He reached out and tilted her face so that he could look into it; her expression was desolate.

''Jenny, love, what is it?'' he asked in quick concern.

She swallowed painfully. ''I'm sorry. I'm grateful for the help with renting the house...truly. It's just...I hadn't thought it would be so soon!'' She gulped and dissolved into tears.

He fished with one hand in a back pocket, took out a huge white handkerchief and used it to mop the face he still held with the other hand. He'd mopped her tears before and brought her out of the doldrums, but this time his gentle care served only to release the floodwaters even more.

It was ten minutes before Jenny sat up and looked at him again. Then she glanced down at his handkerchief and said with a watery little smile, ''I'm sorry. I think I've drowned it.''

''Just wet, not drowned. Feel better?''

''Yes. Lighter, in a way.''

''It's all part of the recovery,'' her doctor assured her with an understanding smile. Soon she was again in complete command of herself. With a brief approving nod, he cleared his throat and asked matter-of-factly, ''Shall I call Blair Graham and tell him to come see you this afternoon, then?''

''Yes, please. I'll be glad to talk to him,'' Jenny answered resolutely. ''There is one thing, though: until I hear from the secretarial agency, I have nowhere to go myself.''

''You will, don't worry. Secretaries as qualified as you are are always in demand.'' He stood up to see her to the door.

"Go ahead and talk to Blair; see what you think of each other. If you both are happy with the idea, you can make a tentative arrangement, depending on your finding a job. He sounded quite determined to stay here a while—I gather he found city life a bit too much for him just now—and he would probably be willing to wait till the house is available. Besides, his aunt will be delighted to keep him with her a little longer, so she can wait on him hand and foot. You know how women love to fuss!"

That provocative remark made Jenny grimace at him, and satisfied with the results of his teasing, he let her go to mail her two remaining letters.

That afternoon, when Blair hailed her from outside the low stone wall around the garden, Jenny was sitting on the grass with a book she hadn't really been reading. She shut it at the sound of his voice, and on her invitation he came through the gate and walked rather stiffly toward her.

As he approached, she began to stand up, but he motioned her back and said with a grin, "No, don't bother. That grass looks like an inviting seat for a spring afternoon." Awkwardly, he lowered himself to the ground beside her. For a minute they simply stared at each other, as frankly curious as two children.

He saw a girl of twenty-one with smooth, dark brown hair that caught the sun in its highlights. Wide blue eyes told him that, in spite of her Cornish name, Jennifer Tremayne had more in her heritage than just the ancient Celts. With an artist's perception he saw also that she was a bit too thin and that the skin around her eyes had a translucent quality. But in spite of that, her mouth had, in repose, the gentle curve of someone whose childhood was happy.

In her turn Jenny saw a big man whose untidy red hair was beginning to be mixed with gray. His eyes were brown and very direct. Around those eyes was a network of fine lines—laugh lines, she suspected—but there were also deep lines around his mouth, which had a certain set look to it when he wasn't smiling. Almost as soon as she noticed it, he smiled again and the fixed look disappeared.

"Well, you don't resemble any landlady I've ever seen, but you certainly pass inspection!"

Jenny laughed and responded with equal bluntness, "And you're not quite what I thought a tenant would look like! Those preliminaries over, would you like to see the house?"

"I would, but I think I'm already making up my mind from the outside." Serene among its flowers, the old house had a look of quiet peace that suited the girl who lived in it and attracted him as a fire attracts a frozen traveler.

Jenny rose easily to her feet, but Blair came to his more slowly and with some difficulty. She looked away to give him a moment; when she looked back, he met her eyes and made a small, rueful gesture.

"That's why I want to stay down here in more tranquil parts for a while. I was in a mountaineering accident a few months ago, climbing for a view. The pieces have all knit back together, but I seem to have gotten very old lying there on my back. I creak, and the city was more than I felt up to handling just now. Aunt Susan offered me a refuge, but I'm a lot of trouble for a dear old lady with arthritis of her own to cope with. Better to have a place of my own if I'm going to stay."

Then he remarked with a twinkle, "Besides, much as I enjoy being fussed over, that's not really conducive to getting any work done." He glanced around again. "And I'm suddenly more eager to paint than I've been in months."

They moved slowly toward the house, and Jenny gave Blair a complete tour. He said very little, only commenting in an upstairs bedroom, "With that north light this would be an excellent studio."

By unspoken agreement they finished the tour back in the garden, where Jenny looked questioningly at her visitor.

"Yes. Houses seem somehow to pick up the personalities of the people who have lived in them. Yours must have been a very happy family, Jenny."

Head bent, she answered in a rather strangled tone, "It was."

He was silent for a moment, studying the slim figure beside him. "I'll be good to it, Jenny. I'll be happy here, too, but whenever you want to pay the place a visit yourself, I can go to Aunt Susan's. You need to know that your home is always here, and I promise it will be."

She looked at him gratefully. "I really can't think you're quite the usual tenant, but thank you for being so understanding."

They agreed on the rent, and Jenny explained that she was waiting to hear from a secretarial agency in London and wasn't sure when she would be leaving the house.

"Not to worry. I'm delighted to have my plans as settled as this, and in the meantime Aunt Susan will enjoy a little more time fussing me to death." He grinned in mock martyrdom.

Jenny walked him to the gate, and with a wave he set off down the lane in his slightly uneven walk. For several minutes she looked after him musingly, and turning away at last, she felt relief that she had indeed found a tenant, and one to whom her home could be entrusted when she herself finally left the village.

CHAPTER TWO

As it happened, it was only a week later that Jenny received the letter determining when she would be going up to London. It was sent not from the secretarial agency but from her father's publisher.

It was a personal letter from David Standish, and the condolences it contained made Jenny blink quickly for a moment. At the end of the letter, though, were the crucial paragraphs:

I thank you for promising to bring us the last of your father's manuscript, Jennifer. Finishing it must have been a difficult thing for you to do, and I particularly appreciate your efforts because I think that this is the best thing Owen ever wrote. It is also beautifully edited; our own editor says that the chapters we already have scarcely need to be touched and arrived almost ready to go to press. There I think I recognize the hand of the secretary Owen bragged about.

That brings me to an important suggestion, Jennifer. You said in your letter that you intended to look for a secretarial position here in London. By coincidence, our Miss Mayfair, who has been with the firm for years, has announced her retirement and bought herself a cottage in Kent to begin what she calls her escape from the city. She promised that she would stay until we found a replacement, so that she could train her successor, but it's been six weeks now and so far we've found no one suitable. She's getting restless and has begun to accuse

us of plotting to keep her here by never finding a
replacement. So, Jennifer, because I've both heard
about you and seen your work for myself, I'm
suggesting that before you look for any other London
position you come here for an interview. I think it likely
that you can help us placate the irate Miss Mayfair.

The letter closed with instructions for locating the offices
of Standish Publishing and a final comment that he would be
looking forward to seeing her.

When she finished reading, Jenny allowed the letter to fall
to the kitchen table, and she simply sat there for a few
minutes, chin in cupped hands. Then she rose and swooped
up her old red jacket from the bench where she had left it.
Although the afternoon sun was warm, the winds along the
cliffs, which were her favorite retreat, would still be cool.

In the garden she slipped her arms into the jacket and,
ignoring the gate, climbed neatly over the stone wall, a habit
that went back to her early childhood. On the far side of the
wall, a narrow path through the gorse wound its way
seaward, and she settled into a steady, graceful walk. Around
her the gorse blossoms spread like a golden fleece across the
stony ground, their sweet scent heavy on the air. But Jenny
was only half-aware of the familiar sights and smells. She
moved automatically, heading for a place she had visited
most of her life whenever she wanted to think things through.

At last she reached her destination, a sun-warmed hollow
along the cliffs, and she settled into it. The sheltering brown
rocks allowed a gentle heat, comfortable and comforting, to
seep into her body as below, waves crashed unceasingly onto
the Cornish coast. Memory quirked the corners of her mouth
for a moment. Years ago from this same vantage point she'd
looked down and seen what she had at first thought to be a
dog, somehow fallen over the cliffs and swimming franti-

cally for its life. She had leaped to her feet, full of wild ideas about rescue, before she realized that the ''dog'' was, in fact, a seal and perfectly content just where it was. With a shamefaced grin for her mistake, she had sunk back into her hollow and watched the seal for long, fascinated minutes before it disappeared. This afternoon, however, no sleek wet head broke through the waves, and Jenny was alone with her thoughts.

Standish Publishing Company. It was one of the best-known publishers of scholarly works in London. Her father had dealt with it for years, and she knew how highly he had respected the firm run by his friend from university days.

The more she thought about David Standish's suggestion, the more interested in it she became. Cautiously she reminded herself that if she failed to get the job, she could contact the secretarial agency again. She decided, however, to go for an interview at Standish Publishing first, without waiting to hear from the agency. She had begun to feel restless the past week, since she'd made up her mind to leave Cornwall and try for a London job. ''If it were done when 'tis done, then 'twere well it were done quickly....'' The quotation from Shakespeare popped into her mind involuntarily, and she smiled a little at its aptness.

Besides giving her a chance to begin work immediately if she proved to be qualified, the job with the publishing company would also offer her a new experience that preserved a link to her father. She knew that for all her hard-won determination to make a new life for herself she would be grateful for a tie to the past and to the parents she still missed so much.

Curled up like a kitten in her warm hollow, Jenny let herself think about her parents more than she had dared recently, and gradually she faced a fact she had not consciously admitted before. The truth was that after her mother's death her father had simply not cared much about living anymore. Not by temperament the sort of person to quit on life—certainly not with a manuscript unfinished—he had gone on working, but when the book was done and the flu worsened, he lost his will to live.

Jenny felt a brief flash of anger at the thought of what seemed to be her father's desertion. Then her innate honesty took over and she conceded to herself that as a reason for living she could not possibly have been a substitute for her mother. Her parents' marriage was a rare kind—a kind she could only hope she would one day know for herself.

Feeling a sense of catharsis, almost as if the steady waves below had somehow washed away the last of her melancholy indecision, Jenny stood up. She was surprised for a moment at a protest from stiffened muscles; then, looking at the golden sun low over the water, she realized how much time her thinking had taken. She had a great deal to do yet before leaving home, but the feeling that she had finally come to terms with the disruption of her life was worth a few lost hours.

She took one last look to the west just as the sun touched the sea and said a goodbye in her mind—a goodbye to the sun, to her favorite place, to her parents and to the sheltered child she had been—then she scrambled off the cliffs and onto the path for home.

TWO DAYS LATER, Jenny pulled the kitchen door shut behind her. Polished and shining, the house was ready for Blair, to whom she'd given a key the previous night. Her cases were in the back of Dr. Pennington's battered station wagon, waiting outside the stone wall to take her into Penzance for the London train.

Reaching the car, she slipped long legs into it, dodging

with the ease of much experience the clutter that overflowed
from the back seat to the front. Then, settled, she met the
searching look the doctor turned on her.

"All right?" he asked.

"Um-hm," she nodded. Both question and answer
referred to more than her position in the car.

He put the old automobile into gear, and soon it was
lumbering through the cobbled square of the village and onto
the road for Penzance. He said nothing more for a little while,
but finally he glanced at her again and noted with admiration
that she seemed calm and composed.

He cleared his throat. "Do you have everything you'll
need?"

"Yes." A small, fugitive smile pointed out that she was
old enough to pack for herself, and interpreting it correctly,
the doctor looked abashed in a way that almost denied his
fifty-odd years. It did not, though, prevent him from
continuing doggedly—perhaps partly so that no more
silences would fall now that his young companion had
presumably said her goodbyes to St. Just-in-Penwith.

"The final chapter?"

She lifted her hands slightly, and he noticed the flat parcel
they held. "*And* I have my toothbrush and my money," she
added with a teasing grin. He grinned back and relaxed
deeper into his lumpy seat, deciding that she would indeed be
all right.

"Well, what can you expect from a Dutch uncle?"

"You're more than that," she countered abruptly.
"You're my oldest and dearest friend, and you're welcome
to fuss over me all you like."

Caught off guard by her words, the tips of his ears turned
pink, and he cleared his throat. As her doctor—and now her
adviser—he had been in and out of her life since the day he
delivered her, dosing sniffles, giving inoculations and even

patching up a broken arm. Having no family of his own, he had become a part of hers, laughing with her mother, playing interminable chess games with her father and teasing her into those ridiculous arguments about everything and nothing. Their affection for each other had always been tacitly understood and now he was touched but embarrassed to have her voice it.

Rushing into words to cover up his feelings, he said, "Tell me more about this letter from the Standish people—the one that's sending you off without your even waiting to hear from the secretarial agency. Not that I don't think your having an interview there is a good idea," he added hastily. "It's just that I don't seem to have had a chance to sit down with you and find out all about it."

She took pity on his embarrassment and followed his lead onto the new topic. "Would you like me to read the letter to you as we go?"

At his nod she burrowed briefly in her handbag, produced David Standish's letter and read it aloud. They discussed his offer, and almost too soon the old car rattled down the hill to the station in Penzance.

He carried her cases onto the train and then, after a sudden tight hug, backed out of her compartment. Soon Jenny was waving out the window to her dear friend as he rapidly dwindled from her sight.

Only then did Jenny turn back into the compartment, which she had to herself for the time being, and take stock. Her father's final chapter lay safely on the seat beside her, and in her handbag was the address of a women's hostel in London, given to her over the phone by Miss Mayfair. In the rack overhead were her two old cases, containing all the clothes she had decided to bring with her.

Those clothes, in fact, had been her only problem in

preparing to leave Cornwall. When she began to pack, she
noticed for the first time that her wardrobe was in sad
condition. The trouble was that she simply hadn't paid any
attention to it since returning home from secretarial college,
and as a result nearly everything she owned was thoroughly
dated. In addition, as she sorted through her clothes she
realized that, without really being conscious of it, she was
selecting all the darker and more somber-looking things.

Her parents would have been horrified at the very suggestion that she might wear mourning for them, but she still
found that the darker colors suited her mood better, and stubbornly she packed them. She knew she'd probably look like a
molting raven in an office full of bright, young secretaries,
but she didn't particularly care. Anyway, these clothes made
her look older, and she rationalized her choice of wardrobe
by thinking that a job hunter should look mature and serious.

She wondered about Miss Mayfair. The woman was
retiring, but the voice that spoke to Jenny on the telephone
had sounded brisk and competent, and Jenny speculated
about the nature of the job the older woman wanted to give
up. David Standish hadn't been very specific about the
position in his letter, but Jenny decided that, in spite of her
years of service, Miss Mayfair must still be in the typing
pool; otherwise, Mr. Standish—kind as he seemed—certainly would not be willing to interview someone as
inexperienced as she herself was.

She also searched her memory—but in vain—for a picture
of David Standish. Although she dimly recalled meeting him
years earlier when her father had decided to deliver a
manuscript in person and brought his wife and daughter to the
city with him, she was unable to remember what the
publisher looked like.

Jenny leaned her cheek against the cool, vibrating glass of
the train window and sighed. Thinking of that trip to London

with her parents had been a mistake. It all came back to her now: they'd had a marvelous time, her parents taking special pleasure in showing her the sights they knew would most delight a little girl. She had seen the Tower of London and the Crown Jewels; watched the changing of the guard at Buckingham Palace; fed the pelicans in St. James's Park; ridden a camel in Regent's Park zoo and gone by boat up the Thames to the red-brick vastness of Hampton Court Palace. The three of them had swung along hand in hand, laughing, and to Jenny now, that vignette almost seemed to summarize her entire sunlit childhood. She braced herself against another of those familiar surges of loneliness and delivered a silent lecture on the greediness of people who have had so much and still want more.

Luckily for Jenny her solitary compartment was invaded at the next of those numerous train stops on the way out of the West Country, and she had no more opportunities to brood. In fact, for most of the rest of the journey to London she found herself caught in the verbal cross fire of a heated discussion on show dogs between the rosy-cheeked little lady who sat beside her and the retired schoolteacher, the tip of his long nose twitching slightly at each emphatic point, who sat across from them both.

Both opinionated parties kept appealing to Jenny for corroboration of their opposing views, but fortunately neither ever remembered to wait for her answer, so she wasn't forced into the dangerous position of taking sides. Instead, she was able to be a spectator and found that both her yearning for the past and her apprehenesion about the immediate future were temporarily forgotten.

When the train finally reached London, Jenny quietly collected her possessions and slipped away from the two combatants, who looked as though they might spend the rest of the night just where they were.

Jenny herself found a cab to take her to the West
Kensington hostel Miss Mayfair had recommended, rented a
single room, and decided to go to bed early so that she'd be
particularly alert the next day for her interview. Unfortu-
nately, her plan didn't work out; she had forgotten from that
childhood visit how noisy the city was at night. After the
sea-softened quiet of Cornwall, the bustling noise of London
made sleep nearly impossible. She lay awake most of the
night, and inevitably her thoughts turned to the past again and
she lost the calm resolution with which she'd begun the day.
Without the silent comfort of her childhood home, which
held so many fond memories, she spent as bad a night as any
since her father died.

The Jenny who appeared the next day at the sleek, modern,
steel-and-glass building that housed the Thames-side offices
of Standish Publishing Company was not looking her best. In
her old gray suit, her eyes shadowed by reawakened grief and
too little sleep, she nevertheless presented herself exactly on
time for her appointment. She had thought about telephoning
in an excuse and catching the first train home to Cornwall,
but the certainty of the discussion such action would provoke
with Dr. Pennington was daunting. Besides, for all his
understanding nature, she didn't see how she could ask Blair
to leave the house he'd just moved into.

Miss Mayfair, who appeared immediately on Jenny's
arrival, proved to be a small, gray-haired woman whose lined
face contrasted with ageless, shrewd but kindly eyes. She
greeted Jenny briskly. "So you're Owen Tremayne's
daughter. I admired your father as a scholar and liked him as a
person." She gave Jenny a penetrating look over gold-
rimmed glasses she didn't seem to need. "I'd enjoy handing
over my job to someone I felt I knew a little about. Let's test
your skills."

And with that no-nonsense introduction she led Jenny into

a small side office and set her up with typing and dictation tests. Jenny found Miss Mayfair's friendly but businesslike manner bracing and knew that she responded to it with a good performance.

"Well, my dear, as I suspected from seeing your father's manuscripts of the past two years, you seem to be an excellent secretary. In addition, although you obviously haven't had a chance to learn about the publishing world yet, you've been exposed all your life to scholarly material typical of what we publish."

She looked at Jenny, who found that she was perched on the edge of her chair. "Yes, you're hired, if you'd care to take the job." Correctly reading Jenny's startled expression, she laughed and added, "As quickly as that! One of the advantages of being older than the company is that I've collected a few special privileges, one of which is the right to hire my own successor. And, as I suspect Mr. Standish told you in that letter, I've been extremely hard to please. Much as I look forward to getting down to my cottage in Kent to begin a life of leisure, I've felt that I simply could not leave until I found the right replacement—and none of those girls they kept sending up from the typing pool was the one."

"But...I'm sorry," Jenny said in confusion, "I thought...I assumed I was being interviewed for the typing pool."

"No, Jennifer." The answer came in a dry tone. "That's years behind me."

Jenny blushed and Miss Mayfair chuckled. "Trust a man to be vague on the most important things! No, my dear, if you accept the job you'll be taking my place as executive secretary to Mr. Standish himself—or rather, to both Mr. Standishes, one in each of those offices off this one."

By now sheer panic was beginning to mix with the

confusion on Jenny's face. Executive secretary to the head of one of London's most important publishing houses? And two Mr. Standishes?

"From the look on your face, Jennifer, I think I'd better go all the way back and start over! Obviously, the situation has never been explained to you.

"For more years than I'd care to count, I've worked for Mr. David Standish, your father's old friend. There is, however, another Mr. Standish here—his son, Adam. For the past ten years, ever since he left Cambridge and decided to enter the firm, Adam Standish has been taking over more and more of his father's responsibilities. As things stand now, he's acting head of the company, and his father comes in only to manage things when Adam is away on business or holiday—just to keep his hand in, he says.

"Now, what we need is an expert secretary to work for Mr. Adam Standish on a regular basis and for his father when the occasion arises. I'll stay on another week or so to teach you the routine and a bit about each man's personal quirks and preferences—they don't notice when we think of these things, but rest assured they'd notice if we didn't!" she added with a laugh.

Jenny gave an answering smile, but her mind was racing. This was a great deal more complicated than she had expected when she'd walked in. It seemed to her as though a job like this would be very demanding, and she couldn't help but wonder if she was really qualified—she who had never worked for anyone but her own father.

"Does that look, Jennifer, mean that you don't think you want the job or that you wonder if you're up to it?" the older woman asked shrewdly.

With a hesitant lift of her shoulders, Jenny said, "It sounds like a fascinating job! I only wonder if I'm suitable for it, with so little experience."

"Your skills are more than suitable, my dear, and I think your personality is, too. Will you trust my judgment when I tell you that I sincerely think you and this job are right for each other?" With a low chuckle, she added, "And I am not simply saying that so I can be off to Kent. I genuinely care about finding the right person to leave my job to, and I think I've succeeded."

Bolstered by her companion's confidence and by a sudden upswing of her own native optimism and fighting spirit—too often dormant in the past weeks—Jenny made up her mind.

"Then I would like the job." She stood up, head high and a smile on her lips. "And if you'll teach me what I need to know, I promise to be a model pupil!"

They exchanged looks of amusement and liking, and Miss Mayfair said, "Good girl! I'll hold you to that, but not until tomorrow morning. In the meantime, why don't you have a look around the city the rest of the day and then have an early night tonight?" She glanced at the shadows under Jenny's eyes and observed tactfully, "You must still be tired after that long trip up from Cornwall. Off with you now, and I'll see you tomorrow morning, first thing."

Lying in bed that night in her little room at the hostel, Jenny felt a good deal happier than she had felt the previous night. She had a job, one that looked extremely interesting; she also had the reassurance of Miss Mayfair's promise to stay until she felt completely at home with the work.

She had spent several hours poring over detailed maps of the city, getting acquainted with its geography and planning some exploratory trips she could make on foot and by subway. In fact, she had even done a little bit of walking already and had begun to feel the excitement of London's teeming life. Loneliness and sorrow would still occasionally be problems, Jenny realized, but she also knew now that Dr.

Pennington had indeed been right again: coming to work in London would be the best possible thing for her.

On that thought she slipped back out of bed and found a sheet of writing paper. Scrambling under the covers again, she wrote a quick note to her old friend, telling him how things were working out. She smiled a little to herself as she wrote; it sometimes annoyed her that he was always right, but she was generous enough to tell him it had happened once again and to thank him for his advice and support.

The letter finished, Jenny put it aside and switched off the light. She lay awake for a while longer, wondering about the next day and in particular about the Standishes, father and son. She was especially curious about Adam Standish, because she would apparently be seeing more of him than of his father. She was conjuring up various possible images for the young publisher when she fell asleep, a faint smile on her face.

A WEEK LATER Jenny looked up at Miss Mayfair, now a trusted friend. "I think you've succeeded. I honestly feel able to cope."

Miss Mayfair's response was prompt. "In that case, let's celebrate and go out for lunch today."

"I'd love to, on the condition that you let me buy you a special lunch in thanks for all you've done for me."

"If you insist, my dear, I'll accept gracefully, but remember what you're already doing for me. Settling into my cottage in Kent no longer looks like an impossible dream, now that I feel so comfortable about turning things here over to you."

They had been busy that week. Miss Mayfair had proved to be a very thorough instructor, and she'd taught Jenny all the necessary office routine. So far, however, Jenny had worked only with David Standish. His son was at the company's offices in Paris, and the older man made brief appearances at the London offices to make certain everything ran smoothly in Adam's absence.

David Standish had come in while Jenny was doing some rather routine typing, and she knew him at once, her memory reawakened. A tall man in his early fifties, he had iron gray hair and a lean, intelligent face. He spoke to her kindly, and when she tried to thank him for suggesting that she apply for the job, he brushed aside her gratitude and turned the tables on her by responding, "My dear, it's I who should be grateful to you. Miss Mayfair has had her faith in me restored and can retire contentedly, and I have the pleasure of knowing that we will still be well taken care of."

He gave her a courtly bow, and Jenny was delighted with his gallantry, knowing she would enjoy working with him whenever he was in the office. On the other hand, how she would feel about working with his son was still an unknown. She had some qualms about not having encountered him yet, and over lunch she worried aloud to Miss Mayfair.

"Nonsense," the older woman said. "But since you're obviously going to fret about your ability to work with him, I suppose I'd better tell you a bit about him, since he's due back from Paris in a day or two."

She settled back comfortably in her chair and, as she did so, glanced up. "As a matter of fact, he seems to be back early."

Jenny wheeled in her chair and, following her companion's eyes, looked across the dining area of the excellent restaurant. At the entrance on the far side, talking to the maitre d', stood the most spectacular couple she had ever seen. The woman looked startlingly like some great cat, her mane of amber hair flowing long and loose over the shoulders of a silky fur cape that topped her gold raw-silk dress. She was perhaps overdressed even for such an expensive restaurant, but the effect was undeniably eye-catching.

That quick assessment made, Jenny allowed herself a long look at the man she would be working with. About thirty, he towered at least six inches over his companion's considerable height and probably would have stood out in any crowd—both because of his height and because of a certain air of command he wore as easily as his impeccably cut light blue suit. From across the room Jenny was unable to discern the color of his eyes, but they were marked by dark slanting eyebrows, and his black hair had an equally distinctive widow's peak. It was a memorable face and at the same time a disturbing one, with a rather feral quality to it.

At that moment the maitre d' led the newcomers to a secluded table in an alcove screened from Jenny's eyes by a miniature forest of potted shrubs and trees. She let out a breath and turned to face Miss Mayfair again.

"*That's* Adam Standish?"

Miss Mayfair grinned openly. "Yes. He inherited his looks from his mother. And I'd have to be at least a hundred years old not to know what you meant!"

Jenny smiled wryly but didn't pursue the topic of his looks. Instead she asked, "Do you know who the woman is? She's lovely."

"No, but that isn't surprising. He always seems to be escorting someone new, and the women he escorts are always beautiful."

She looked at Jenny, then said in a suddenly brisk tone, "Are you finished, my dear? If so, let's be on our way. I doubt if Adam Standish will be in the office before tomorrow, but there's a possibility he'll stop by today, and I want to be completely certain you're at home with all our office procedures before I leave and you have to deal with him on your own."

Jenny had begun to collect her handbag and light coat, but

at these last words she looked up with a return of the apprehensive expression she had worn earlier.

"Now don't start looking worried again," Miss Mayfair admonished with a chuckle. "I'll be here until the end of the week when I'll go out in a blaze of glory at the retirement banquet that's traditional for us oldtimers. Then I'll be off to my lovely cottage, but by then I'm sure you'll be fine. Adam Standish is a demanding employer, but never an unfair one."

It was one of those perfect spring days, and they walked in comfortable silence back to the building that housed the company's offices. Just before they reached the main door, Miss Mayfair slowed her pace for a moment and looked indecisively at Jenny.

"I never got back to telling you about Adam. I've known him since he was a little boy, and now I'm wondering how much I should tell you about him to help you understand the grown man."

Perhaps it was a legacy of her father's gentle reserve that made Jenny say slowly, "Perhaps nothing is best. After all, I'm only going to be his secretary, and for that it doesn't seem to matter whether or not I understand him as a person."

Later she would wince, remembering that cool pronouncement, but now she met Miss Mayfair's questioning look calmly as they entered the building.

CHAPTER THREE

THE RETIREMENT BANQUET was a great success. The Standishes, father and son, sat one at each end of the long table, with Miss Mayfair sparkling to the right of the courtly David Standish. She insisted that Jenny, who so far had had little opportunity to meet anyone else, should sit on her right, and Jenny gratefully accepted the place, glad of the woman's support one last time. Miss Mayfair and the elder Mr. Standish saw to it that she was included in their conversation, and at this safe distance from the younger Mr. Standish she was able to relax and enjoy herself.

Once, however, she happened to glance down the table just as he looked up. Their eyes met, then he lifted his glass in a silent but mocking toast. She turned quickly away again, wondering what it was about the man that rattled her.

By then she had worked with him for three full days, taking over complete responsibility as his secretary while Miss Mayfair simply remained in the background, ready to help if anything Jenny couldn't handle should arise. Nothing did, and Jenny found to her relief that she was perfectly capable of dealing with his correspondence and appointments—both business and social, as he seemed to draw no line between them and expected her to arrange the timing of his activities both on the job and off.

His eyes that, at closer range, had proved to be a strange light gray, had watched her intently while she worked that first day, almost, she thought to herself with an edge of irritation, as if he expected her to prove less than competent. The second day, however, he seemed satisfied with her abilities and relaxed slightly, even going so far as to toss her a casual compliment on her speed and accuracy in dealing with his letters. That being the case, she wondered why she still felt tense and nervous whenever he was near.

She puzzled about it briefly during a lull in the conversation, then mentally shrugged. She was doing her job effectively and he seemed satisfied with her work; that was all that should matter.

Then kindly David Standish, so much less disturbing, spoke to her, and Jenny abandoned her analysis of his son's effect on her. When her glance later slipped down the table again, Adam was talking to the attractive woman on his left; to judge by the absorbed expression on her face and the way she occasionally laughed, he was an excellent conversationalist when he chose to be. Jenny didn't look in that direction again.

On Sunday afternoon she saw Miss Mayfair off on the train for Kent, knowing she would miss the friendly little woman who had taught her so carefully. The older woman gave Jenny a quick hug in parting.

"You'll be fine with David Standish, bless his heart, and don't let Adam fluster you, just because he happens to be as handsome as Lucifer," she said with a shrewd twinkle. "And remember, there will always be a spare room ready for you if you want to escape from the city and spend a weekend with me."

With a final wave Miss Mayfair darted into her compartment and was gone.

Making her way back to the women's hostel in Kensington, Jenny thought over those parting words with a rueful smile. Perhaps she was susceptible to Adam Standish's attractions because she had met so few young men at home, living a life that she now saw had been unusually sheltered. In fact, the long hours she had spent in the company of her father

and Dr. Pennington might explain why she was so at ease
when David Standish was in the office and so edgy when it
was his son who managed things.

At any rate, she promised herself, Adam Standish was
never going to know that he interested her in the slightest.
She would be the perfect secretary, coolly efficient and
completely impersonal. She was an employee of Standish
Publishing Company and had no time to waste wondering
about her employer as anything but an employer.

DURING THE NEXT FEW WEEKS Jenny stuck admirably to her
resolve. She was prompt, efficient and so quiet she might
have been a well-oiled machine. She appeared at the office
each day in her sober, slightly unfashionable clothes and
worked conscientiously, making little contact with other
employees, except for an occasional word at lunch with
women from the typing pool. Her position as secretary to the
two Standish men, however, seemed to set her a little apart
from the others, and she made no real friends among them.

She might have felt thoroughly lonely, but she was still
busy adjusting to life in London, spending almost every
moment of her free time exploring. She had quickly learned
to read the colorful maps of the city's superb subway system
and delighted in using it. On an impulse she decided that she
would get to know London by disembarking at every stop in
the system and seeing what each area of town was like. It was
a project she knew would take a long time to complete, but
she enjoyed working on it slowly and methodically. Her
knowledge of the city grew steadily, as did her affection for
it.

She also received regular letters from Miss Mayfair, who
seemed, much to Jenny's pleasure, determined that their
friendship continue. The letters were entertaining, written in
the slightly acid tone Jenny knew well, and humorously

detailing her attempts to become a country woman after a lifetime in the city.

Dr. Pennington wrote occasional notes, too—hasty scrawls on whatever scraps of paper came to hand. Even Blair Graham wrote once, to tell her that the house was being well cared for. It was a funny little letter illustrated with tiny sketches of himself washing floors and pulling weeds. Jenny laughed, as he had meant her to, but was grateful for the kindness that had prompted him to let her know all was well with the only home she had ever known.

Only a few times in those weeks did her determination not to think of Adam Standish in any personal way waver, and her occasional lapses seemed to result from the plentiful evidence she had of his busy social life. Although her infrequent work for David Standish included only letters and a few business appointments, her work for Adam required her to do a great deal of those things, as well as act as his social secretary. Often he casually asked Jenny to see that flowers were sent to one address or another, and she made a number of reservations for dinners, concerts and plays. A few times, while she waited with telephone in hand for conformation of Adam's arrangements, her mind wandered, and she had to haul it back from idle speculations about what an evening in his company would be like.

One of those times, much to Jenny's embarrassment, Adam walked quietly from his office into hers and discovered her with a dreamy expression on her face. She hastily rearranged her features into something more businesslike and saw one swooping eyebrow lift in amusement. She pinked with the suspicion that he had read her mind, but after enjoying the sight of her flushed cheeks for a moment more, he sauntered back into his own office, hands nonchalantly thrust in his pockets, without even saying what he had wanted. She finished her call in as brisk a manner as she could manage, then went into Adam's office to tell him of the arrangements for the evening.

He sat at the polished expanse of his desk, engrossed in a folder stuffed with papers, and Jenny's wayward mind made note of the fact that the bent head was extremely well shaped. Her voice was cool, however, as she told him about the arrangements, and without looking up he murmured, "Thank you, Miss Tremayne. I'm sure that will be fine."

There was nothing more to be said on the topic, so she returned to her own office, only half-conscious of a vague feeling of disappointment.

It was a few days later that Jenny finally began to realize something about Adam's active social life. She had just put a call through to his office when the outer door opened and a woman glided in, a woman just as spectacular in her way as the beautiful lioness Adam had been with the first time Jenny saw him.

Like a valuable china shepherdess, this woman was tiny and perfect, from the top of her coil of glossy black hair to the tips of her green French-kid shoes. Her skin had the mat texture of a flower petal, delicate color blooming high on her cheekbones. She wore an off-white suit with a high cowl collar that set off the fine line of her jaw, and her rose-tipped fingers were pulling off a pair of green kid gloves as she moved toward Jenny with a graceful swaying walk.

More conscious of her own dated clothes than she had ever been before, Jenny collected herself and rose to meet the apparition.

"Good morning. May I help you?"

Eyes that tilted slightly at the outer corners looked her slowly up and down, and a voice that was low pitched and a little husky said, "So you are the new Miss Mayfair. Will you stay here, serving faithfully and bloodlessly, until you are as old as she?"

Startled, Jenny managed to murmur only, "Yes, I'm Miss Mayfair's replacement." The rest of the outrageous remark she ignored.

"Mr. Standish is on the telephone at the moment. May I—"

"No matter. I will wait in his office anyway." Her small head held high, she walked imperiously toward Adam's closed door.

Doubtful but unable to resist that air of command, Jenny moved quickly enough to reach the door first and swing it open. With a tiny inclination of her head, the woman swept past Jenny and into the room.

Adam looked up from his telephone as they entered, and at the sight of his visitor his eyebrows shot up. He smiled at her, and with his free hand beckoned her to a chair. She ignored the gesture, however, only tossing onto the chair the cream-colored handbag into which she had tucked her gloves. Then she began to prowl around the room, swaying gracefully across Adam's handsome Turkish carpet to pick up and put down a small jade horse and then study the admirable view of the river far below. She ignored Jenny completely and seemed content to wait until Adam was finished with his call.

Adam looked up at Jenny, still hestitating at the office door. Having reassured himself with a quick glance that his visitor's back was to him, he responded to Jenny's helpless palms-up gesture with a resigned shrug and a swift conspiratorial grin that surprised her. Then, while concluding his phone conversation, he nodded his head slightly toward the door, indicating that she should go.

As the door closed behind her, he put the receiver down and Jenny could hear a rustle of fabric and a husky voice cooing, "Adam darling, are you not glad to see me? I have come to take you to lunch with me."

Jenny slowly crossed her own office and sank into the chair with a puzzled expression on her face. What had Adam, always so cool and mocking toward her in the past, meant by that look?

She had little chance to wonder, though. The inner door opened, and the two strolled across Jenny's office, Adam looking rather remote, the woman on his arm looking complacent.

"Miss Tremayne," he said distantly, "I'm going to lunch with Madame DuBellay. Please see to things until I get back." And then they were gone, leaving Jenny at her desk where she read herself a lecture on the folly of becoming too interested in the activities of one's boss.

But the conclusion she drew from that particular episode, a conclusion reinforced over the next week or so, was that much of her boss's activity was apparently not initiated by him. Previously, she had just reported his personal phone messages without paying any attention to them. Now she couldn't help noticing that usually those messages offered invitations with such a mixture of command and plea that it would be nearly impossible to refuse them with any courtesy.

As well, Jenny discovered that although Adam never arrived late at the office the mornings after these engagements, on the contrary setting himself as demanding a schedule as that of the least of his employees, he sometimes came in looking particularly taut, his lean face somehow more angular than usual.

On one of those mornings, a Monday, Jenny answered the telephone to hear the remembered husky voice of Madame DuBellay demanding to speak to Adam. Pulling together her courage to resist that demand, Jenny courteously asked her to hold the line for a moment and put down the receiver before a refusal could be voiced. Instead of ringing through to Adam's office, she knocked quietly on the door and entered in response to a muttered, "Come in."

Shutting the door behind her, Jenny leaned against it for an instant and looked across the luxurious office at Adam. He sat at his desk, head bent, and didn't look up at her immediately. When he did, she saw tiny lines of strain etched around his eyes. Somewhere inside Jenny a little catch hampered her breathing.

"What is it, Miss Tremayne?" he asked wearily.

"I'm sorry to disturb you, Mr. Standish, but Madame DuBellay is on the phone, and I thought perhaps I should check with you before I put her call through."

He looked at her coolly, one of those dark eyebrows raised, and said, "Rather interfering of you, isn't it?"

Instantly a flaming scarlet, Jenny almost didn't hear his next words over the roaring in her ears. "But you were right, Miss Tremayne, and I thank you for it."

The words sank in slowly, and Jenny's frozen posture thawed, while her face returned to its normal color and her hearing cleared. He was looking at her now, not with irritation or even irritation masked by courtesy, but with an expression that for once was not mocking. Instead, he wore a rueful smile.

"It's probably another luncheon invitation—or should I say command—and I thank you for offering me a few minutes' protection!"

Cautiously, Jenny returned his smile. "Are you available to speak to her?"

He didn't answer right away but sat curiously intent, studying her. Then the slightly satiric look she knew well came back. He rose from his desk and faced her with the tiniest sketch of a bow.

"Will you forgive a lack of chivalry in the invitation, my dear Miss Tremayne, and promise to have lunch with me, so

that I'll be unavailable to the lovely but difficult Madame
DuBellay?''

Masking her reaction, Jenny responded smoothly, picking
up his tone to perfection, ''Why, of course, Mr. Standish.
Since you're my employer, your wish is my command.''

He grimaced slightly, acknowledging her thrust, but said
only, ''Thank you. And now if you'll put through that
call...?''

He sank back into his chair, and Jenny whisked neatly out
the door, closing it with what might have been exaggerated
care. At her own desk she picked up the receiver, apologized
to Madame DuBellay for the delay and told her she was
putting the call through, then connected it to Adam's phone.
That done, she sat bolt upright, drumming her fingers on the
top of her desk.

She was seething, full of swirling protests. How dare he
invite her out just to protect himself from his lady friend?
He shouldn't be taking his secretary out to lunch anyway;
the old taboo on mixing business with pleasure was simple
common sense. But if he had to do it for protection, couldn't
he at least have used some polite fiction to conceal the real
reason for his invitation? Not that she would have been
deceived. After all, she hardly expected him even to notice
her, when he was so accustomed to the dazzling women he
habitually escorted. But he might have had some regard for
her pride!

Furious, she beat a tattoo on the desk and didn't even
notice when the light on her phone went out, indicating that
Adam had hung up.

Only when his door opened did she look up, to find him
propped negligently against the jamb. He studied her
outraged expression for a moment, his own face inscrutable,
and said, ''Shall we go at one?''

The ''perfect secretary'' snapped, ''Yes, if you like.''

"I do like." He smiled very slightly and moved quietly back into his office.

IN HER HOSTEL that evening Jenny finally allowed herself to think about her lunch with Adam. She made herself a cup of tea on the hot plate she'd bought, and then, wearing her old, plaid wool robe, curled up in her one big chair, cradling the steaming mug for warmth.

He had taken her by cab to a small French restaurant in Chelsea. Its decor was unremarkable, and its service friendly rather than elegant, but the food was unquestionably the best Jenny had ever eaten.

She left the menu selection to Adam and covertly studied his face while he spoke with the waiter. The morning's lines of tension were gone, and he looked startlingly attractive, his dark coloring thrown into contrast with the light brown of a perfectly cut suit and an immaculate cream-colored shirt. When he finished with the waiter he turned and caught Jenny's look. One mobile eyebrow shot up and he asked sweetly, "Do I pass inspection?"

She blushed a little, unaware how becomingly the color warmed her skin and brought it to life; then she folded her hands and said primly, "You look very nice, Mr. Standish."

He laughed outright, the first time Jenny had seen him do such a thing, and she saw that it served only to make him more attractive.

"Surely, Miss Propriety, you can spare me the 'Mr. Standish' treatment out of the office!"

She smiled in response to his teasing but shook her head. He tilted his for a moment and took note of the carefully composed way she was sitting and the slightly nervous look in her eyes. Then he settled down to make himself so charming she would forget her qualms.

He succeeded admirably. He led a conversation that

ranged over so many topics that later on Jenny couldn't recall what they had talked about. What she did remember was that he was so witty and engaging a speaker that he had completely broken down her shyness, and in turn she had responded with more conversational skill than she'd thought she'd possessed. When the food arrived, she ate absentmindedly, only a small corner of her mind observing that it was the best meal she had had in some time.

It had finally ended, though, and they rode back to the office in silence. It was not an uncomfortable silence, however, but one produced by a feeling of companionship. When they reached Standish Publishing, Adam led her to her desk and seated her, then with a lift of an eyebrow, expressed his thanks for her delightful company and walked into his own office. He shut the door, and Jenny didn't see him for the rest of the afternoon. When she rang through at half-past five to tell him she was leaving, he said only, ''Good night, Miss Tremayne,'' and she left with a sense of anticlimax.

Now Jenny finished her tea and set the mug down, wrapping her arms around her knees. The truth was that she simply didn't know what to think. Adam had begun the whole thing by calling her ''interfering,'' had infuriated her by using her as a social dodge, and then had treated her as if she were the most important woman in his life. What on earth was she to make of all that?

She puzzled about it for a while longer, then gave it up as incomprehensible. To escape her thoughts, she rooted out some paper and sat down to write Miss Mayfair an entertaining letter that mentioned nothing whatsoever about lunching with her employer.

CHAPTER FOUR

ARRIVING AT THE OFFICE in the morning, Jenny hung up her light coat and wondered how Adam would behave after yesterday's luncheon. Her question was answered almost immediately. Adam arrived a few minutes later, said a brief "Good morning" and called her into his office to take dictation. He rattled off seven letters, and she had to call on all her skill to keep up. When he finished he said, "Do those immediately, please, Miss Tremayne. I'd like them to catch the morning mail."

Without a word Jenny returned to her desk and began typing. She worked furiously, rapidly but accurately, trying not to hear a voice in her mind say, *Well, that's that*.

But it seemed to be true. During the next two days Adam worked hard and kept Jenny working at the same pace. His behavior was completely impersonal, and their delightful lunch together might never have happened. To herself Jenny admitted that she was hurt, but she retained enough common sense to know such a feeling was foolish. Adam had needed a lunch companion, just as he needed a typist, and the one made her no more important to him personally than the other.

On Wednesday afternoon when she called through to his office to tell him she was leaving, Adam said, "Right. Oh, by the way, Miss Tremayne, I'll be at the Paris office for the next two days, and my father will come in to keep track of things here."

There was no expression in his voice, and he offered no explanation of why he hadn't told his secretary about the trip earlier. Glad that he couldn't see the disappointed look on her face, Jenny answered in the same colorless tone, "Yes, sir. Have a good trip."

"Thank you," he replied and hung up.

She scooped up her coat and purse and left the building as quickly as possible. On the sidewalk in front she hesitated a moment, then decided to walk home rather than use the subway. She set off, striding purposefully as if to belie the confusion in her mind. Why should she care so much that he was making a trip to the Paris office and she wouldn't see him again until the following Monday? After all, despite that lovely meal they'd shared, it was hardly as if she were anything more to him than a handy piece of office furniture; certainly, that was the way he had treated her since Monday!

Storming along as she was, Jenny hadn't noticed that a light rain was falling. She became aware of it only when a sleek, dark green Jaguar pulled in to the curb beside her and Adam's voice called, "Hop in before you're soaked." She paused, and as a car came up behind him and honked, his words became a command. "Come on, girl!"

She slipped obediently inside and quickly settled herself on the rich leather seat, wondering inconsequentially if it would become spotted from the water on her coat. Adam pulled smoothly out into the traffic and asked, "Where do you live?"

She gave him the address in a tight little voice and sat staring straight ahead. He glanced quickly at her once, then concentrated on his driving.

When they pulled up in front of Jenny's hostel, he parked the car and came around to open her door. As she stood up, he looked at the worn, gray building and said, "So this is what Miss Mayfair recommended. Are you comfortable here?"

"Yes, thank you, I'm fine," she answered primly. Then curiosity got the better of her. "How did you know Miss Mayfair suggested it?"

He angled a small smile down at her. "I asked her to be sure you had somewhere safe and respectable to live."

"But why should you care where your secretary lives?"

"Because I do," was the terse answer as he took her arm and escorted her to the door. When they reached it, he waited a moment to be sure she had her key, then said, "I have to be off to the airport. Good evening." As she lifted her face to wish him good night, he suddenly bent and kissed her forehead. Then he was gone.

Jenny groped her way inside the dark entryway as the green car purred away. Would she ever understand the man?

AFTER HER THREE DAYS of emotional turmoil, Jenny found Thursday and Friday restful. Working with David Standish had none of the tensions of working with his son. The older man was as efficient as the younger, apparently able to pick up exactly where Adam had left off, but he gave Jenny none of the feeling of harried confusion his son did. Instead, he treated her with a grave, old-fashioned courtesy that almost denied an employer-employee relationship. They worked together harmoniously and effectively, both conscious of a quiet mutual liking.

On Friday afternoon he asked her to put through a call to his home in Surrey, and a few minutes later he asked her to come into his office.

"Jennifer, my dear, if you have no special plans for this weekend, my wife and I would very much like to have you spend it in Surrey with us. I can't promise you peace and quiet," he added with a laugh she would understand later, "but the countryside is lovely this time of year."

"Why, thank you," Jenny murmured, her mind racing. She had planned nothing but more solitary exploration of London; foremost among her thoughts, however, was a surge of interest in seeing where Adam came from. She knew, of course, that he had a house somewhere in the city, but instinctively she guessed that the place where he grew up would reveal far more about him. Completely forgotten was her remark to Miss Mayfair that she didn't need to know what influences and forces had made Adam the person he was.

"Will you come, then?" David Standish's kind voice spoke into her scurrying thoughts, and Jenny decided hastily.

"Yes," she replied, smiling. "I'd love to."

"Good! Shall we treat ourselves to an early quitting time, so that I can drive you home to collect whatever you need for the weekend?"

Dimpling suddenly at the roguish look that accompanied his suggestion of an early escape to the country, she ran to get her coat and bag.

The drive to Jenny's hostel was far more comfortable than the one two days earlier. They talked easily of trivial matters, and Jenny was able to relax with the father in a way she could not do with the son. At the hostel it took her only a few minutes to throw together a few clothes: her one dinner dress that was still reasonably stylish, a shirtwaist dress, a skirt and matching sweater, nightclothes and makeup. On a last-moment inspiration, she burrowed in the small closet and dug out an old pair of jeans, a warm pullover and heavy shoes. These, too, were bundled into her suitcase, and Jenny flew back out to the waiting car.

The trip to Surrey was beautiful. Absorbed in adjusting to a new place, a new job, a new life, Jenny had paid little attention to anything not directly within her sphere. Now, driving out of the city in David Standish's large, comfortable car, she looked around, amazed to see that spring had turned into summer. After that first sleepless night in London, she had quickly become accustomed to all the noise and bustle, but country bred, she found herself basking now in the sunlit peace of Surrey.

True, the docile lawns of the country were far different from the untamed wilds of Cornwall; still, after the city's clutter the open spaces made her feel strangely at home. Perhaps it wasn't surprising, then, that her thoughts turned to St. Just and her parents. What was a bit surprising was that David Standish seemed to share those thoughts. He spoke into the companionable silence.

"You know, Jennifer, I was glad to count your father as a friend, and I admired him enormously as a scholar, as well. It seemed to me sometimes as though each book he wrote after we left university was better than the one before. Certainly this final book—which should be out in about six weeks, by the way—is superb. The subject of those early saints of Britain is one that normally would be of interest to only a limited audience. He treated it, however, with so much warmth and simplicity, in spite of such scholarly material, that it should appeal to all sorts of readers. I'm proud to be publishing it."

In the weeks since leaving Cornwall, Jenny had come to terms with the loss of her parents, remembering them with love but able to live her own life. A rare wave of sadness broke over her now, mixed with gratitude for David Standish's words. Unable to speak for the moment, she thanked him with a look.

Catching the glance and reading it correctly, he cleared his throat and went on. "I'm also glad to have you working for us, for a variety of reasons. It pleases me to have Owen's daughter in my company—especially when she's such an excellent secretary!"

He gave her a quick smile and saw her pleasure at the compliment, then continued, "I'm grateful to Adam for suggesting, when your letter came, that we interview you. He pointed out to Miss Mayfair and me that we already knew your secretarial skills were formidable and also suggested that you might be happier working at something that had a connection to everything you had known. I think more slowly than my son,'' he added ruefully, ''and by the time I'd worked that out in my mind, you would probably have taken a job somewhere else.''

This time he didn't see Jenny's reaction; eyes on the road ahead, he missed the way she started when he mentioned his son's role in hiring her. Adam had not only thought about housing her in London but had also had the original idea of suggesting that she apply for the job! How could she reconcile this type of swift, intuitive kindness with the image she tried to cultivate in her mind of a mocking, unpredictable socialite?

Fortunately, they were coming up the hill into Guildford, and David Standish was too busy pointing out the town's seventeenth-century guildhall clock, hanging far out over the busy street, to note Jenny's confusion. Or if he did notice, he was too tactful to let her know.

They worked their way through Guildford, and Jenny caught a quick glimpse of the town's handsome brick cathedral before the car turned onto a narrow road that ran roughly parallel to a small tributary of the river Wey, flowing between gently green banks. Finally they crested a gentle rise and slowed before the entrance to a long driveway. Through the molten-gold light of a perfect summer afternoon was the most beautiful house Jenny had ever seen. The sight of it nearly took her breath away and drove all uncomfortable thoughts from her head.

An Elizabethan country home on a small scale, the house was surrounded by gardens: flowers and fanciful topiary in a formal garden; a small knot garden; scattered fruit trees and a large kitchen garden of vegetables and herbs. Rising from the midst of this cool greenery, the rose brick of the house seemed to catch the warmth of the slanting sun while the mullioned and oriel windows caught its light, creating a glittering display. Small corner towers marked the traditional H-shape that was a compliment to Henry VIII, and a smaller central tower contained a clock. The balanced symmetry of the towers was, however, contradicted by the whimsical clusters of chimneys, tall pipes with bricks that somehow formed fantasies of rope and lattice and chevron designs.

Jenny released the breath she had inhaled some time ago and turned to her companion, to find him looking not at his beautiful home but at her pleasure in it. He grinned boyishly at her rapt expression and said, "I know. It always affects me that way again when I've been away from it for a few weeks."

He put the car into low gear and started down the long winding driveway, going very slowly to give Jenny a chance to admire each new angle of the building. As they went, he told her a bit about the house's background.

"It was built in the late sixteenth century by an English corsair, one of the gentlemen pirates the first Elizabeth licensed to prey on Spanish shipping in the New World. He enriched both his queen and himself, and with his share of the plunder built this house."

He paused and chuckled. "Supposedly he built the house on a small scale so that Elizabeth could *not* come and stay here when she and her court went on a progress through the countryside. Having her as a guest was a great honor but a financial catastrophe—she often stayed until her host's food and money ran out—and our man seems to have been very pragmatic about preserving his fortune! At any rate, this is one old house where I can promise you'll find no beds that Elizabeth slept in. Perhaps that's why he named the house Repose: secure in the knowledge that the queen would not be arriving, he must have found life here very restful after the excitement of piracy on the Spanish Main."

Jenny's intent look was proof of her interest, so he went on. "Since those days the house has changed hands a number of times, as the fortunes of its owners rose and fell. When the publishing company had just begun to be a success, this place came up for sale for the first time in many years, and I had an opportunity to buy it partly furnished. I gambled that the company would go on being a success and bought it for Adam's mother. I had to go to the city every day, sometimes stay there during the week, but Adam spent nearly all of his childhood here."

An odd edge had come into his voice and Jenny, despite her enthrallment, noticed it. She made no comment, however, except to murmur, "What a lovely place to grow up."

"Adam thought so, and most of his time here was very happy." The edge had become more pronounced, and his hands seemed to be gripping the steering wheel more tightly. There was silence in the car for a minute, then he spoke again and his hands relaxed their hold a little.

"These days, with Adam doing most of the work in the city, I can stay here and enjoy my house and family. That includes, by the way, the twins, Geoffrey and Joan, and the smallest member of the household, Teddy, as well as my wife, Anne." Now his voice was full of warmth again, and Jenny recognized with a tiny pang the signs of a family as closely knit as hers had been.

Before she could think any more about it, the car drew up at last in front of the house, and David Standish came around to help her out. Meanwhile, from the house poured what appeared to be a positive swarm of people, and Jenny was swept inside to the great hall with its magnificently carved golden oak paneling.

Soon the swarm resolved itself into distinct shapes. The pretty and surprisingly young dark-haired woman whose arm was linked affectionately with David's was his wife. She greeted Jenny in a warm voice and freed her hand to squeeze the younger woman's. "I'm delighted to meet you, Jennifer, and even more pleased David was able to talk you into coming here."

"It didn't take much persuasion," Jenny admitted frankly, and Anne laughed.

"Good! I only hope spending a weekend with our brood doesn't frighten you off ever coming back."

At that she reached out and nudged the children into a small line, which held just long enough for hasty introductions. The freckle-faced and brown-thatched twins, wearing identical striped jerseys and jeans, looked to be about ten, and the small, round blond figure who sucked gravely on the battered leg of a toy lamb was two-year-old Master Teddy. Then the line dissolved; the twins ran her case upstairs and went back to whatever they had been up to—probably no good, their mother guessed ruefully—and Teddy-and-lamb ambled over to David. His father swooped him high on his shoulder and, laughing with Teddy's happy crowing, said, "I'll take this one upstairs and get him ready for bed while you two get acquainted."

They then disappeared up a shallow, sweeping stairway, and Anne and Jenny exchanged looks of amused understanding.

"Would you like to see a bit of the house before supper?" Anne asked. Jenny agreed with pleasure, and Anne led the way through the sun-filled and, at the moment, quiet rooms.

Jenny's sense of the geography of the house rapidly failed her, but she was at least able to build a sort of cumulative impression. Carved-oak wainscoting and mantelpieces combined with high plaster ceilings to give the rooms a feeling of airy warmth. The furnishings were a pleasing mixture of Elizabethan and Jacobean pieces, with their carved wooden solidity, and more modern ones, with their soft padded depths. The effect was of a comfortable hodgepodge: this was no sterile showpiece, but a lived-in and much-loved family home.

They finished their tour in an upstairs bedroom off the long gallery. Tall windows and sparse furnishings lent the room a spacious look, and Anne showed Jenny the modern bathroom, tucked into a large closet. The bedroom, with its own paneling, carved chimneypiece and a heavy Jacobean chest between the big windows, was in period decor except for the modern four-poster bed that had replaced an Elizabethan one.

Anne smoothed its handwoven spread with a house-wifely hand and smiled at Jenny. "I hope you'll find this room comfortable. We do have two of the old beds that came with the house—complete with hangings as well as carving all over their headboards, footboards, posts and even canopies! But they're more for look-ing at than sleeping in. We've found they tend to give us claustrophobia, so we don't imprison guests in them.

"Supper will be in about an hour, Jenny, and while you're getting settled I think I'd better go see why the twins are so quiet—that's usually a bad sign!"

With a laugh she was gone, and Jenny walked to an open window. Her room looked down on the formal garden, and the sweet pungent smell of box, released by the day's warm sunshine, wafted up to her. She breathed in deeply, taking in also the quality of serenity that surrounded her—in spite of the twins' shouts, faintly heard from a distance. With amusement she wondered what Anne had found them doing. Leaning against the window frame, Jenny also wondered about Adam; what relationship did he have with this beautiful home and loving family?

No immediate answer presented itself, and she stayed at the window, almost mindlessly absorbing the sensations around her until she finally turned reluctantly away to get ready for dinner.

CHAPTER FIVE

FOR JENNY the weekend was an almost enchanted escape from the pressures of living in the city and working with Adam Standish. Already comfortable with David Standish, she soon counted Anne as a friend and was accepted by the children as an overgrown ally.

Even though a light rain fell almost all day Saturday, nothing dampened their spirits. The twins lured Jenny into games up and down the long upstairs gallery and dragged her off to their special lair, a tiny secret room enclosed by massive brick chimneys, while small Teddy annexed her with sticky, trusting fingers whenever she came within reach.

Breathless and laughing, Jenny reveled in it all. While David and Anne looked on and teased, she entered into romp after romp. Not that far removed from childhood herself, she found that she loved children and had a natural affinity with them, even though she had been an only child.

Once, catching her breath between games by the high-backed sofa where Anne and David sat watching the uproar in comfort, Jenny made a laughing apology for being so uncivilized a guest.

"Nonsense," David returned with a grin, looking more relaxed and younger than he had in the city. "We haven't laughed so much in months, and the children adore you. Besides, you're saving our weary old bodies from their onslaughts!"

He shot a quick look at Anne, who stuck out her tongue at him, then added, "Really, Jenny, as well as being a relief for us, it's a treat for them to have you here. They get tired of having just family around during the school holidays, and you're a delightful break in their summer routine.''

At that moment the twins pounced on Jenny again for ''just one more game,'' and at David's off-with-you gesture she allowed herself to be hauled, chuckling, away.

Sunday they all attended church in Shere, and Jenny was hard pressed to recognize Teddy, dapper in a tiny sailor suit, and the twins, awkward in their Sunday best. When they reached home, however, the children metamorphosed immediately, while the adults changed more slowly into casual clothes, Jenny pulling on the old jeans and red pullover she'd brought. The weather had cleared, and by unanimous agreement they decided on a picnic lunch in the garden.

Jenny helped Anne put the meal together in the big, white, old-fashioned kitchen. The older woman explained that while she had daily help with the other housekeeping chores, she loved to cook for her family herself.

Certainly she put together a delicious meal with a minimum of effort, unearthing cold chicken, fruit, biscuits, half a cake and bottles of wine and fruit juice. The twins were recruited to carry everything outside, where Anne spread a white cloth under the trees.

They ate until they were stuffed and sleepy, then lounged lazily on the grass. David read the Sunday papers and sat with a curl of smoke twisting up slowly from his pipe, while Anne produced some embroidery and worked on it in a half-hearted fashion. The children heaped themselves on and around Jenny, and in the murmuring summer afternoon everyone drifted off to sleep.

Some time later Jenny heard the sound of tires on gravel, but she wasn't really awake until a cool, mocking voice nearby said, ''Well, if it isn't Miss Tremayne.''

She sat up with a lurch, dislodging arms and legs that lay

trustingly over her and provoking sleepy protests from the children. There stood Adam Standish, hands in the pockets of another well-cut suit, both eyebrows lifted as he looked down at her tousled hair and rumpled clothes. Startled blue eyes met distant gray ones that apparently held no memory of their parting. He did not look especially pleased to see her there.

Jenny was too stunned to say a word, but fortunately David pulled himself from behind his crumpled newspaper and said calmly, "Hello, Adam. So you *were* able to stop by on your way in from Paris. Glad to see you back."

Hastily pushing her dark hair out of her eyes, Jenny looked quickly at David. Did that mean he knew when he invited her to Repose that Adam might be coming there? Forgetting for a moment he was the senior member of the company where she worked, she glared at Adam's father, but he only returned her look with a bland smile.

He did, however, save her from further contact with Adam for the time being. Putting out a hand, he had Adam haul him to his feet and began to ask about business affairs at the Paris office as the two strolled toward the house.

In spite of Jenny's movements, the children slept on like a litter of exhausted puppies. Anne, too, had lain motionless beside her abandoned embroidery while Adam was near, but now she opened eyes that were fully alert.

Too upset to be entirely polite, Jenny rounded on her. "Did you know Adam would come here today?"

Anne studied her flushed face for a moment, then said, "No, Jenny. David didn't tell me." Seeing Jenny's look of puzzlement at her answer, Anne sighed and sat up to wrap her arms around her knees. With a glance at the sleeping children, she continued quietly, "David doesn't tell me much about Adam's doings, nor Adam much about mine. I'm David's second wife, and Adam's stepmother, even though I'm only nine years older than he is. David divorced

Adam's mother when the boy was thirteen; she lived in Italy for a few years and died there when Adam was sixteen. David married me two years later.

"Adam refused to come to our wedding, saying he wanted nothing to do with it. Perhaps he was overreacting emotionally; he was at a good age for that when we married, but he's never changed his attitude in the years since. I guess it's just become a habit."

She paused for a moment, glancing abstractedly at the house and gardens around her. "I've never really understood the problem, but I think perhaps it ties in somehow with this lovely house and Adam's idyllic childhood here. Maybe he missed the growing tensions between his parents, and their divorce came as a stunning blow to him—all the more horrifying because he'd been so happy himself. He couldn't accept the divorce at first, blaming David because he was a handy scapegoat and then blaming the mother who never again made any attempt to see him, even though he had adored her.

"I've sometimes thought," she added musingly, "that this explains Adam's attitude to most women. Judging by the society columns of the papers, he leads a very active social life, but each time I see his picture he's with a different woman, and he's always wearing that sardonic expression. It's almost as if he's willing, up to a point, to use them as decorative accessories to his life but essentially dislikes and distrusts them. Certainly that's his attitude toward me!"

The look on her gentle face was almost bitter, then she reached out one hand to smooth the soft baby hair from Teddy's pudgy, sleeping face, and her expression softened. "Oddly enough, though, the children don't seem to figure in Adam's resentment of our marriage. He's good with them, and they adore him; they're delighted on the rare occasions he comes down here to talk business with David—the only reason he ever does make an appearance! Whenever I'm about to despair of Adam, I remember the way he is with the children, and that gives me a bit of faith that someday he'll be able to accept me, too. I hope so. I know the division in his family bothers David.''

She looked thoughtful for a minute more, then with a sudden deliberate change of mood plucked a blade of grass and used it to tickle cheeks and noses of the sleeping children. As they sputtered awake, she prodded them to their feet.

''Come on, you lazy lot! Much more of this sleeping in the daytime and I'll have a tribe of howling insomniacs on my hands all night, heaven forbid!''

Not entirely certain what insomniacs were, the children nevertheless responded to her teasing tone, and with a certain amount of tucking in of rumpled jerseys and scratching of tousled heads they wandered off through the garden in search of entertainment, one twin on each side of Teddy.

With loving amusement Anne watched them go, then turned back to Jenny, who had been listening so intently to what the other woman had been saying about Adam that she had forgotten her own dismay and embarrassment. That might have been partly Anne's intention. At any rate, she smiled at Jenny and said easily, ''Shall we dispose of the remains of the picnic and see what we can find for a quick tea before you have to leave?''

Jenny agreed, and once inside Anne made the tea with her usual efficiency, sending Jenny up to pack and change into her blue shirtwaist. Then Standishes of all sizes were rounded up to eat again.

Anne's words about Adam still echoing in her mind, Jenny noticed now that beyond the bare essentials of politeness he hardly spoke to his stepmother, although he laughed with and teased the children, allowing them to scramble all over him, dribbling crumbs as they did so. He quickly looked the worse

for wear, but the children's chatter and clatter got the adults
over the first few awkward minutes together.

David did his share, too, talking easily and humorously as
if completely unaware of the tensions between Adam and the
women. Such naturalness made it easy for the others to
follow his lead, and soon Jenny saw Anne relax into her chair
and felt her own taut muscles ease.

The twins wandered off when their voracious appetites
had been appeased. Teddy, on the other hand, was
perambulating the room, and when he reeled over to her
chair pleading ''Cake, Jen-ny?'' she scooped him up and
popped a bite into his baby-bird mouth. Laughing over his
ruffled head, she was able to meet Adam's thoughtful stare
calmly.

''The children seem to have an advantage over me in the
business of names, Miss Tremayne. Out of the office may I
be allowed the freedom of your first name, too?''

The words were scrupulously polite, but Jenny thought she
heard an undertone of something in his voice. She was
looking at him rather doubtfully when David spared her the
necessity of answering right away.

''Actually, I suspect that none of us have been calling
Jennifer by her real name. Am I right, Jenny, that it's really
Guinevere?''

''Yes,'' she admitted in surprise, ''but how on earth did
you know? Thanks to my father the old form is on my birth
certificate, but mother and I were able to persuade him from
using anything but the new form of the name—except to
annoy me.''

David laughed. ''Don't be annoyed with me for letting it
out, please!''

Then he added, ''Funny the things you remember. When
Adam spoke, I suddenly thought of your father back in
university days, deep in the old texts of the Arthurian

romances, saying that if he ever had a daughter, he'd name her after King Arthur's fair queen. So he did it!''

He looked at Jenny inquiringly. ''I always thought 'Guinevere' had a lovely sound, but I've forgotten what Owen told me it meant.''

''It's from Gwenhwyfar, Celtic for white wave.'' In a small voice, she added, ''He liked to say that I came into their lives like a joyful wave breaking on the Cornish coast.''

''How beautiful,'' Anne said softly, and Jenny looked at her gratefully.

At that point Teddy, still on Jenny's lap, surprised everyone by asking, ''How did I get named?'' and the moment's poignancy evaporated. His mother, from the next chair, chuckled and said, ''You were named, my darling boy, for the Teddy bear whose shape yours greatly resembles!''

His attention caught by the phrase ''Teddy bear,'' Teddy ignored the laughter of the adults and slid off Jenny's lap to go in search of his chewable lamb.

By mutual consent the others stood up, and the subject of names was dropped without Jenny ever answering Adam's question. As he rose from the shadowy corner where he had been sitting, Adam gave her a look that implied clearly he still wanted an answer but would let it pass for the time being.

Instead, he turned to his father and said, ''Since I'm going back to London tonight myself, shall I save you a trip and take Miss Tremayne back with me?''

Jenny thought of time spent with Adam in the closeness of that luxurious green car, and her mind shouted a silent ''No!'' just as David's voice said a pleasant ''Yes.''

Adam nodded briefly and said, ''I'll get your case, Miss Tremayne,'' before he strode out of the room.

His father took Jenny's small hands in his and smiled down at her. ''I hate to let you go at all, my dear, but since you must

I suppose Adam's idea makes sense. We thoroughly enjoyed your company, though, and I'll look forward to seeing you again, either here or at the office the next time Adam's out of town!''

Anne came forward, also, and flashed her husband a look of mock reproach at that last remark; then she turned to Jenny and said warmly, "The children and I would love to see you, too, Jenny, whether or not Adam goes out of town. Now that we know you can survive the confusion we live in, we'd hope to make you a part of it often!''

Adam returned to say that the car was ready out front, and Jenny moved to the door with the two men while Anne went in search of the children. When she returned, herding them in front of her, Jenny gave each a quick hug. From Teddy she received the approximation of a kiss that had more feeling than accuracy, and from the twins two hasty pecks. Then Anne kissed her and David took her hand for a moment, before Adam helped her into the car. He shook hands with his father, flicked the children's hair affectionately and bade Anne a cool goodbye. Then they were off.

Jenny craned her head around for a last look as they moved down the long driveway. A variety of hands waved goodbye, and behind them in the dusk, golden light spilled out of the open door. Adam tooted the horn, and then they topped the rise at the end of the driveway and the house vanished from sight.

With a little sigh Jenny faced front again, wondering what she could possibly find to say to Adam during the drive up to London. Her cautious opening gambit was, "I liked your family tremendously.''

He answered curtly, "Yes, I noticed.'' Then silence fell again. There didn't seem to be anything else to say on that subject, and for the life of her Jenny couldn't think of another. For a moment she studied Adam's hands on the steering wheel—big hands, with wide palms and long, capable, blunt-tipped fingers—then switched her gaze to the window beside her. In the deepening twilight she watched Guildford pass by, its lights winking on gradually, but soon the constant sideways motion of things along the road dazed her eyes. One object blurred into another, and Jenny drifted off to sleep, thus escaping her conversational problem.

A few minutes later, traffic slowed briefly, and Adam used the opportunity to look at Jenny. With an expression that was a blend of exasperation and amusement, he noted that she slept deep in the rich leather of her seat with the abandon of a child Teddy's age, her lashes fanned out over the smooth line of her cheeks. Cloudy dark hair spread across the collar of her old trench coat, and her small hands lay limply in her lap.

Then the traffic sped up again, and as they rounded a corner she slipped, with a tiny murmur, against his shoulder. With his right hand Adam reached around her to settle her more firmly against him, his fingers slipping through the soft waves of her hair as he did so. Like a kitten Jenny rubbed her cheek against his hand without waking; then the hand was gone, and Adam drove steadily through the darkness toward London.

CHAPTER SIX

WHEN ADAM FINALLY STOPPED his car on the quiet side street in front of Jenny's hostel, he switched off the engine and simply sat for a few moments until the quiet and lack of motion woke her. She sat up stiffly, and before she had time to realize in what position she had been sleeping, he stepped out of the car and came around to help her out.

Jenny swayed slightly as she stood, and Adam steadied her with one hand, pulling her case out of the back seat with the other. Then he slipped his arm over her shoulders and led her, unprotesting, around the back of the car and up the walk.

At the front door she fumbled for her keys while Adam put the small case down beside her. He looked at her, blinking vulnerably up at him, touched her cheek with the tip of one finger and murmured, "Sleep well, little one," then swung away down the walk. Still bemused, Jenny peered after him until the sleek green Jaguar pulled away. Then she stumbled sleepily inside and up to bed without ever completely waking.

She went in to work the next morning wondering if Adam would mention anything about finding her as his father's guest at Repose. He said nothing about the weekend, though, merely giving her a brief rundown on his time in the Paris office and asking her how things had gone in the London one. She brought him up to date in a few sentences, saying as she finished, "Your father is very easy to work with."

At that he gave her a quick sideways glance and asked, "Could that possibly imply I'm not?" He gave her no time to formulate a tactful answer, but immediately began dictating letters. Jenny had to hurry to keep pace.

The rest of the day was equally busy, and it seemed to set a pattern. Adam worked more efficiently than ever, and he assumed that Jenny would stay abreast; with some effort she did. She dragged herself home each evening, but he seemed inexhaustible, actually stepping up the pace of his social life. During the next few weeks Jenny made numerous dinner reservations, arranged for many concert and theater tickets and sent flowers to a variety of addresses—Madame Du-Bellay's and others.

Madame DuBellay herself appeared twice at the office, once at lunchtime and another day late in the afternoon, to enlist Adam as her escort. Both times she paid Jenny about as much attention as she would pay a piece of furniture, apparently feeling that the girl was of less than no importance.

As far as she was concerned, Jenny was able to derive a certain wry amusement from being the ''invisible woman,'' but when Adam walked out with nothing but a curt ''I'll see you tomorrow, Miss Tremayne,'' it was harder to be philosophical. She stubbornly refused to speculate why that should be true.

Then, one Friday afternoon some three weeks after her visit to Surrey, Adam called Jenny into his office just as she was gathering her things to go. When she walked into the room, he was standing at the far window looking down at the river below, his hands in his pockets and his back to her.

Hearing her step, he swung around and looked at her for a thoughtful moment, then said abruptly, ''Miss Tremayne, will you have dinner with me this evening?''

Jenny's pretty mouth fell open and then shut like a bewildered fish. He seemed to find that amusing, and a quick genuine smile lightened a face where shadows had been only a minute earlier. His voice suddenly more youthful, he said persistently, "Forgive the short notice and do come, please."

The notice *was* too short, implying that she had nothing better to do with her time than accept a last-minute invitation from him—which was true, but he shouldn't assume it. Also, she still felt that a boss shouldn't be taking out his secretary. And besides that, she had nothing in her tiny hostel closet she'd be willing to be seen in, out for dinner with Adam Standish. All of these things being true, Jenny said yes.

"Good. Shall I come for you at eight?"

She agreed distractedly, her mind flying ahead to the number of things that needed doing before eight, then sped out of his office without even remembering to say a temporary goodbye. He chuckled quietly as he watched her go, then heard the outer door slam behind her.

Out on the sidewalk Jenny thought hastily. She couldn't go out for dinner in anything she had, so she'd simply have to get something new immediately! She'd spent little of her generous salary since coming to work at Standish Publishing, and her savings account also contained the rent money Blair Graham regularly sent up from Cornwall. For the first time in months, Jenny was interested in shopping for clothes.

She was lucky. When she reached the hostel an hour and a half later, she was juggling a miscellaneous collection of boxes and bags. Gasping her way up the steep stairs to her room, she burst in her own door just as the entire pile slid out of her hands. With a breathless little laugh, she kicked the door shut and gathered up her bundles, spreading their contents across the narrow bed. After a quick happy inspection, she was off down the corridor for a bath.

She was too excited to think about being fashionably late; besides, she had a shrewd suspicion Adam would have scant patience with that tactic. By a quarter to eight she was ready and pacing her small room, glad it looked onto the street so that she could watch for Adam.

She knew she looked attractive, but that was, in fact, an understatement, although Jenny herself wouldn't have known it. She had piled her glossy, fresh-washed hair high on her head, leaving a few soft tendrils loose to curl along the nape of her neck. Her chiffon dress had long, full sleeves and a fitted bodice with a V neck, while the knee-length skirt fell in graceful folds from a high waistline. The fabric's delicate Dresden blue color made her skin look like fine porcelain and her eyes like early violets, but Jenny didn't see that, knowing only that it became her and that the dress had "belonged" to her from the moment she'd tried it on in the boutique. She wore tiny sandals on her feet and a fine gold chain of her mother's around her neck, but no other ornament. On the chair by the door lay a little satin evening bag and a lovely velvet evening cape of a deeper blue; Jenny had splurged on it, knowing how deplorable her old tweed or her trench coat would look over the chiffon dress.

She was at the window when Adam pulled up, his elegant car looking incongruous in front of the old hostel. By the time he reached the outer door, she had flown down the stairs and was there to meet him, her excitement evident in flushed cheeks and sparkling eyes.

He couldn't miss the glow on her face, and he was far too well acquainted with women's fashions not to know that she had been on a special shopping trip. He was, however, also far too tactful to make so much of her looks as to imply that she was ordinarily anything less than well dressed. He merely said, "Good evening, beautiful Guinevere"—at which her flush deepened becomingly—and taking her arm, escorted her down the walk to the car as if she were indeed of some ancient royal line.

Aside from recalling that they had both felt young and

happy, Jenny couldn't afterward remember many details of the evening, beyond the bare facts that they ate at another of those excellent restaurants Adam knew and attended a symphony concert. Then they stopped briefly at his house in Ennismore Mews for the coffee and sandwiches that the couple who worked for him had left by a warm fire in his library. But the entire evening was for Jenny blurred by a sort of fine shimmering haze.

There was one thing she did remember clearly, and would all her life. That was the moment—driving home through the streets of London—she turned to look at Adam's clear-cut profile, silhouetted against passing lights, and realized that she loved him. He must have heard her sudden little intake of breath, for he reached out his left hand and covered both of hers for a moment as they lay in her lap. He said nothing, however, for which Jenny was grateful since she would have been unable to respond coherently.

When they stopped in front of Jenny's hostel, they still hadn't spoken again, Adam, too, perhaps being in a thoughtful mood. He handed her gracefully out of the car and walked her to the door. Reaching it, he waited while she found her key, then he took her in his arms. She came unresisting.

He looked at her face, white in the lamplight, and then kissed her full on the lips for the first time, his own lips firm and vital. Clinging to him, Jenny responded mindlessly, only a tiny corner of her mind able to note with surprise the depth of feeling he aroused in her. It might have been a minute or an hour later when he raised his head slightly, whispered "Thank you" with his breath warm against her lips, and released her. He was gone before her vision cleared.

Reaching her room somehow, Jenny undressed like a sleepwalker and hung her lovely dress and cape in the tiny closet. In the cold bathroom at the end of the hall, she unpinned her hair and let it fall around her face—a face that in the mirror seemed to belong to someone else. Absentmindedly, she went through the motions of washing and returned to her room, crawling into the hard little bed and lying there on her side, cheek propped on her hand. She meant to think over the evening and come to terms with the discovery of her feelings for Adam, but she was able, before she fell asleep, only to get as far as deciding that her employer mustn't find out that his "perfect secretary" was in love with him.

To Jenny it was the beginning of a sort of double life. On the one hand, she was the efficient secretary who handled Adam's calls and correspondence and who arranged the details of the busy social life he continued; on the other hand, she was the bright-eyed girl who sometimes went out with him herself, dressed in clothes she couldn't resist buying for those occasions.

She tried not to think too much about the situation, but often couldn't help but be disturbed by it. For the sake of both of them she felt she should say no to his invitations. The acting head of a large London publishing house shouldn't be seen escorting his secretary, and that same secretary shouldn't be indulging in a love for her employer that had no possible future.

And she was convinced it had no future. Adam usually kissed her good night when he dropped her off, and she couldn't help responding to the touch of his lips, but he never spoke a word about loving her. Mindful of what Anne had said about his attitude toward women, she guessed despairingly that he never would speak any such word and resolutely closed her own lips on the stream of endearments she longed to pour out whenever he was near. But she couldn't seem to refuse his invitations.

One Wednesday in early September Jenny answered the telephone to hear a well-remembered voice.

"Good afternoon, Jennifer."

"Miss Mayfair! How nice to hear from you! Would you like to speak to Mr. Standish?"

"No, my dear, I'd like to speak to you. What are you planning to do on your birthday?"

"Birthday?" Jenny repeated blankly.

"Yes, Jennifer, birthday. Yours. It's on Saturday, I believe," came the dry rejoinder.

"I'm sorry to sound so vacant," Jenny apologized, "but I had completely forgotten about it." Then she asked, "But how did you know?"

A small chuckle came over the wire. "It was on that form you filled out for me to submit to the personnel office, and I made a note of it at the time. Now tell me, my dear, have you made any plans yet for this weekend?"

"Why, no," answered Jenny, who had been wondering between hope and apprehension when Adam would issue the next of those irresistible invitations.

"In that case I would love to have you come down here and spend the weekend with me. Kent is very beautiful at this time of year, and I'd like to show you a bit of it, beginning with my cottage."

"And I'd like to see it. Yes, thank you, I will come."

"Excellent!" Miss Mayfair exclaimed in pleasure and went on to give Jenny instructions on the best way to get to her place.

Jenny put the receiver back in its cradle thoughtfully. She had accepted Miss Mayfair's invitation almost without thinking and realized now that she had been responding to a sudden urge to escape—to get away from London and all the complications produced by Adam Standish's presence.

With a wry little quirk of her lips, Jenny remembered Miss Mayfair's original broad invitation in the spring, to come for a visit if she wanted a break from the city. Both of them had thought then that she might want to escape from the pressures of work, but in fact she would be escaping from the pressures of love. Whatever the reasons for her flight, though, she was grateful to Miss Mayfair for offering a sanctuary, and she knew she would enjoy seeing the capable little woman who had already become such a good friend.

On Thursday morning Jenny lifted her head as Adam finished dictating some letters and found him looking at her with the suggestion of a smile lurking in his eyes.

"Would you have dinner with me on Saturday, Miss Tremayne?"

Jenny stood up, ready to return to her own office, and without quite meeting his eyes said coolly, "I'm sorry, Mr. Standish, but I'll be out of town this weekend."

"Oh?" The trace of a smile was gone.

"Yes, I will," Jenny returned with a flash of asperity, annoyed by something in his tone.

"But why this weekend?"

Goaded by his inquisitorlike manner, she snapped, "Because it's my birthday, and I choose to spend it with a friend! And now if you'll excuse me. . . ." Without waiting to hear if he would, she swept out of the room.

The rest of the day they saw little of each other, and both were scrupulously polite the times they did meet. Jenny was thankful when she could leave for the day, but of course she had to come back in on Friday, and they continued to be as distant as if they had never seen each other outside working hours. Jenny was distressed by it but kept reminding herself that the mere fact of his being her employer did not give him the right to grill her about her off-duty activities.

She was dimly aware that there was something inconsistent in her being so annoyed with Adam just because he wanted to take her out to dinner, but she refused to recognize why this was so.

Late that afternoon Jenny left her office briefly on an errand, and when she returned there was a package on her desk, wrapped professionally in heavy gilt paper. Puzzled, she opened it. Inside, with a note that simply said, ''Happy birthday—A.S.,'' was a bottle of perfume. She freed it from its wrappings and stood it on the desk, an ostentatiously large crystal flagon of heavy gardenia scent—the sort of thing he was probably accustomed to buying for Madame DuBellay, Jenny thought in mingled distaste and disappointment. Could he really see no difference between her and his lady friends? If not, she would far rather have received no present from him at all.

Ready to leave for the day, she rang through to Adam's office. ''I'm going, Mr. Standish. Thank you for the perfume,'' she said in a flat little voice.

''You're welcome. Have a good weekend, Miss Tremayne.''

She made a small, inarticulate sound and clicked off, then left the office quickly. She didn't know that Adam sat staring at his closed door for a minute before walking to the window where he could see her far below as she left the building.

In spite of its inauspicious beginning Jenny's birthday weekend was pleasant. After a brief stop at her hostel to pick up the case she had packed the previous night, she caught a train south from Victoria Station, then took a bus the last four miles into the village of Smarden, once the site of one of the many ''dens'' or clearings the ancient Saxons had carved into the forest of Kent.

In the village itself Jenny followed Miss Mayfair's directions, walking past the church and a cluster of Tudor houses, then turning along a lane that ran near the river Beult. Without difficulty she found the cottage she sought, neither new nor very old, and there was Miss Mayfair, waiting impatiently for her arrival.

They exchanged a hug, and Jenny was given a steaming cup of tea, followed by a delicious light supper. Over it they chatted casually and, in general terms, Jenny told her friend how things were going at Standish Publishing. She said nothing about her feelings for Adam Standish, or about their occasional dates, but Miss Mayfair noticed a certain slight tension in Jenny whenever Adam's name was mentioned. She did not comment on it, however, only thinking to herself with shrewd kindliness that it was probably a good thing that she had brought Jenny out of his orbit for at least a weekend.

On Saturday the two women enjoyed a leisurely walk around the village, Miss Mayfair indicating points of interest with a local pride that she admitted was increased by sentimental association. Her grandparents had lived in the village when she was a little girl, and she affectionately remembered seeing the sights herself while walking hand in hand with her grandfather.

Certainly Smarden had several noteworthy attractions for the visitor. As well as the beautiful, old, half-timbered homes, many with thatched roofs, there was the village church of St. Michael, with its crenellated towers and broad expanse of oaken roof, suspended unsupported, it appeared, from side to side of the ancient building. Jenny was also particularly intrigued by the tall, white-tipped, cone-shaped kilns, inside which Kent's famous hops—Miss Mayfair pointed out the heavy clusters ripening on the vines—would soon be drying.

She also brought out her venerable Mini and drove Jenny to Canterbury, knowing how much her guest would enjoy it. They retraced the route of Geoffrey Chaucer's pilgrims in *The Canterbury Tales*. Like those visitors of old, Jenny stood in the mighty nave of Canterbury Cathedral, which was filled with soft gray light and scattered bouquets of color from the stained-glass windows. She visited the famous Norman crypt, with its solid ponderous vaulting, and in the nearby transept saw the stone that marked the spot where, in December of 1170, Thomas à Becket, archbishop of Canterbury, was murdered by knights of Henry II.

Spellbound, all other thoughts driven from her head, Jenny was lost in history, seeing in her mind's eye the frightened townspeople come to dip bits of torn-off clothing in Becket's blood and proclaiming miracles wrought with those relics. She could visualize King Henry, penitent at last for the death of the man who had once been his friend, humbling himself at Becket's bier, barefoot and flogged by Becket's monks. She saw more than three centuries of pilgrims like Chaucer's, drawn by both piety and wanderlust to the tomb of Saint Thomas, chief shrine of England until the sixteenth century, when, during the Reformation, Henry VIII destroyed the shrine and apparently the martyr's remains.

Miss Mayfair had left Jenny to wander through the cathedral by herself, and on the way back to Smarden the younger woman was very quiet, her thoughts still lost in past centuries. At last, with a little sigh, she turned to her friend and said, "Thank you for taking me there. I've wanted to see Canterbury Cathedral since I was a child, and it certainly didn't disappoint me."

Gratified by Jenny's pleasure, her friend replied, "I'm glad to have been able to give you that experience, my dear."

She also gave Jenny a lovely paisley scarf that evening. Stroking its soft folds, Jenny looked up from her birthday present with eyes that were brighter than usual. "You're such a dear friend to me! Thank you."

"I'm enjoying myself," Miss Mayfair answered rather gruffly, "so thanks are completely unnecessary, Jennifer."

On Sunday they attended services in the village church, affectionately known as the "Barn of Kent" because of the unusual open construction of its roof, and after dinner Jenny caught a bus for the train station and London. Refreshed by her time away from the city, she kissed Miss Mayfair fondly, feeling grateful she had regained her perspective. Even Adam's gift now seemed more amusing than distressing.

As it happened, when she walked into her office Monday morning another package lay on her desk, and sounds from Adam's office indicated that he had come in early. With a quick, irreverent grin, Jenny hoped it wasn't more impossible perfume. Then, as she picked up the heavy flat package, she saw a note in Adam's handwriting that said only "the first copy" and, suddenly eager, tore away the wrappings. In her hands lay her father's final book, magnificently bound and printed, and as she leafed through the pages Jenny, misty-eyed, saw the familiar passages.

Holding the book tightly, she knocked on Adam's door and entered. He looked up, one eyebrow raised inquiringly, then stood just in time to receive his "perfect secretary" in his arms. She'd forgotten herself and hugged him, the book still clutched in her hand.

"Adam, thank you so much! It's beautiful, and there's nothing I'd rather have. Thank you for understanding how much the first copy would mean to me," she said breathlessly.

With a smile he said, "You're very welcome, Guinevere," and kissed her lightly before she freed him and returned to her own office. Adam looked thoughtfully after the girl who had thanked him so differently for his two gifts.

CHAPTER SEVEN

ADAM NEVER ASKED about Jenny's weekend, and for reasons she herself didn't really understand, she never told him about it or that the anonymous friend was, in fact, Miss Mayfair. The beneficial effects of her time spent away from him stayed with Jenny for a while, but inevitably they began to fade as she and Adam slipped back into their pattern of occasional dates and Jenny had to concentrate on concealing the fact she cared for him more than he did for her.

This uncomfortable situation continued until, on a crisp October evening, Adam drove her to an old converted mill in the country for dinner. Throughout a delicious meal, which Jenny in her turbulent state of mind barely tasted, Adam was as witty and charming as was his custom when they were outside the office. Jenny had to force herself to respond in kind.

Over coffee, however, they both fell silent, Adam watching the hot liquid swirl in his cup as he stirred it, and Jenny sitting quietly, tired by the strain of hiding her emotions. Suddenly he put his spoon down with a clatter and raised his eyes to look at her. She kept her own eyes lowered, and he simply studied her for a minute, noting that in repose her mouth fell into a weary little line and that even the warm rose of her wool suit didn't put any color into her cheeks.

"Guinevere, will you marry me?"

The words came quietly across the table, and Jenny didn't seem to hear them. She sat motionless for a long moment, then raised her bewildered gaze to Adam's face, searching it wordlessly. She found no answers there; his expression was strangely unreadable, but she continued to stare at him while a tumult of thoughts shouted in her mind.

Loudest was the one that asked "Why?" Why should he ask her to marry him? Adam, who distrusted women as anything but temporary companions; Adam, who if he did nevertheless choose to marry, could take his pick of the glamorous socialites of London. Did he ask her because she was a change of pace from the rest of the women he knew, or because he knew his father liked her and would welcome her into the family? Or—worst of all—did he ask her out of pity because he had somehow guessed her feelings for him?

At that last humiliating possibility, the chance of joy stillborn, her face must have changed, because Adam abruptly broke the silence. Harshly he said, "Don't look so dismayed, Jenny. This isn't meant to be a tragedy!"

He paused and moved his water goblet—a random gesture by a hand whose knuckles were white. "I didn't intend to distress you," he said, his voice still roughened, "but I seem to have done so anyway, and I apologize.

"I asked you to marry me because I thought we might make a tolerable success of it. Model secretary though you are, you should have a home of your own, something more than a little room in a shabbily respectable women's hostel! As for me, maybe I'm getting past the age for the playboy life I've been leading; I find more and more often that it both tires and bores me.

"We don't know each other well enough for loving—" in her lap Jenny's fingers twisted her napkin into a rope "—but we seem to have liking, and perhaps that's a better foundation for marriage. God knows," he added bitterly, "my parents loved each other madly when they married, and that didn't stop their marriage from ultimately being a catastrophe! I don't expect some adolescent notion of domestic bliss, but I think we could get by in relative comfort. I would be busy with the company a great deal of the time, of course, and you would be free to develop interests of your own.''

The napkin knotted tightly through her fingers, Jenny sat quietly while Adam spoke, frantically fighting a desperate urge to stand up in the middle of the restaurant and shriek at him to stop. When he finally did, rather like a clock that had, at last, run its spring down, she sat frozen in her chair, gazing blindly across the room. She noticed none of the low murmur of the other diners around them, hearing only a sound in her ears that was almost like the tinkle of delicate crystal shattering.

What could she do? She knew he was waiting for her answer. How could she marry a man who said plainly that he didn't love her and offered only what an earlier generation would have called a marriage of convenience? Yet, how could she refuse to marry a man she loved with all her heart, regardless of his lack of feeling for her?

When she brought her eyes back to Adam, her thoughts still racing, he had turned his own head and was looking through the window by their table. In the autumn darkness it was difficult to see much of the picturesque mill pond beyond the glass, but he didn't turn back to meet her gaze, and Jenny was able to study his profile.

She knew and loved his features, but now her close scrutiny revealed things she had never seen before. Lines had begun to cut deeply down his cheeks and at the corners of his mouth, and his thick black hair showed threads of white at the temples. One long-fingered hand lay beside his coffee cup, but even at rest it had a certain tension.

''Adam . . .'' Jenny spoke across the gulf.

He finally turned back to her with eyes that seemed possessed of the shadows from outside.

''. . . Yes.'' And a tiny flame leaped in the shadows.

SEVERAL WEEKS LATER Jenny was on a train for Cornwall and home. Adam had come to the hostel, which she left without regret, collected Jenny and her luggage and driven her to the train station. He saw her into a first-class compartment and stowed her cases overhead, then fished a sheaf of the morning papers out of an overcoat pocket and gave them to her. That done, he bent down in the compartment Jenny still had to herself, brushed the soft hair from her forehead and kissed her lightly. He straightened and began to turn away, but Jenny leaped to her feet and called him back.

He swiveled to face her, and she moved to him, putting both small hands on his chest and stretching up her face to kiss him with a determination that rather surprised them both. He seemed almost to hesitate an instant, but then he held the two little hands tightly against him and kissed her breathless. Afterward he freed himself, said softly, ''It will be all right, Guinevere,'' and jumped down onto the platform. In a minute the train pulled out and he was lost to her sight.

Jenny folded herself into her seat, staring out the window as London's backyards passed before her unseeing eyes. Dimly she heard the train's clanking, syncopated rhythm of steel on steel, and the regular sound sank hypnotically into her thoughts, which drifted back over the time since her acceptance of Adam's extraordinary proposal.

They had said little more on the subject that first evening, and for a time they kept on working together impersonally during business hours. Adam took Jenny out more often, though, and she found she'd stopped making arrangements for his social life as he'd ceased seeing other women.

Only Madame DuBellay seemed to take strenuous objection to this, in spite of considerable tact on Adam's part. She called repeatedly and finally quarreled with him on the telephone so loudly that Jenny, padding quietly into his office with letters for him to sign, could hear her voice, shrill now rather than husky, say, "That little nothing? Ridiculous!" Then Adam cut in with a firm goodbye and hung up the phone. Jenny's cheeks were pink, and he said ruefully, "I'm sorry you heard that, Guinevere. The lady is no lady."

Jenny just shook her head with a small smile, put down the letters and left the room. Back at her own desk, though, she dropped her head in her hands for a minute, and that was the way Adam found her when he came quietly in with the signed letters. He put them on her desk, then reached over and, with cool fingers, tilted her chin so that she had to look at him.

"I shall marry whom I choose, Jenny, and I choose to marry you. I'll be a great deal more comfortable with my Cornish 'goodwife' than with that London 'fishwife.'"

One of the winged eyebrows was up, and Jenny managed a smile at his gentle mockery. He noticed the lingering strain in her face, however, and said perceptively, "Shall I phone the family at Repose and ask if we may visit? I think we have news that will please them."

As he had intended, the suggestion distracted her, and she agreed happily. She often had mixed feelings about accepting Adam's proposal—a remote little voice of self-preservation warning her she was on a primrose path to heartbreak—but one unqualified joy was that marriage to Adam would make her part of a family she already loved.

He reached past her for the telephone on her desk and put through the call to Surrey, leaning casually on the edge of the desk in a position that brought him so close to Jenny her heart started to pound. Eyes lowered, she lectured herself furiously on the idiocy of being disturbed by the nearness of a man who didn't love her, even though he was planning to marry her. So intent was she on resisting the attraction of Adam's closeness that she missed his entire conversation on the phone, looking up only as he replaced the receiver.

He seemed to be blandly unaware of their proximity to each other, standing up easily and saying, ''Well, that's all set. We'll go down Friday evening for the weekend. Those monkey twins come home from school on the weekends, so we'll have to face the whole family at once. Think you can stand the strain?''

She laughed and nodded her head, but in the lovely green car late Friday afternoon she wondered if, in fact, she could. She had no fears about the reactions of David and the children, but what about Anne? It was Anne who had, in effect, cautioned her about Adam's attitude toward women. Would she be pleased or worried by their news? Would she see it as a long-awaited thawing on Adam's part or reckless risk taking on Jenny's? Or worse, would she—observant as she was—realize that for Adam this would be a marriage without love? Anne's own warmhearted nature would probably be repelled by that, and Jenny flinched at the thought.

In spite of her fears, however, the visit had gone well. They arrived at Repose just in time to be dragged in for supper by the twins, and before they were able to finish eating those same children were demanding to hear the promised news. Adam resisted briefly, but they closed in on him from both sides, Joan putting his plate out of reach and Geoffrey removing his glass.

''All right, all right,'' he agreed with a wistful glance at the remaining morsels on his plate. Then, putting down his napkin, he stood up and stretched across the table to retrieve the glass from Geoffrey's clutches. He raised it and looked around the table at the collection of expectant faces. ''A toast to Miss Jennifer Tremayne, soon to be Mrs. Adam Standish!''

With a flourish he drained the glass and sat down, while the storm broke around Jenny. The twins flung themselves on

her with confused cries of "A wedding, Hurrah!" and "Can
we be in it?"

Laughing, Jenny said recklessly, "Yes, of course," and
the pair released her to begin practicing immediately: Joan
paraded up and down the room in what she took to be a stately
fashion, while Geoffrey followed her with an imaginary and
very heavy train. Meanwhile, Teddy scrambled into Jenny's
lap to present her with a wet kiss; what for, he wasn't quite
sure, but that didn't stop him. David took her hand in a strong
clasp and said warmly, "My dear, you're making us all very
happy."

And finally Anne, too, came over to Jenny. Removing
Teddy, she handed him to his father, then kissed the younger
woman. She said only, "Adam is very lucky, and so are
we," but the look in her eyes was enough to make Jenny's
throat close a little as she returned Anne's embrace.

Adam had sat detached from the hubbub, snatching the
chance to finish his meal and watching the confusion he had
created with what, to Jenny's eyes, appeared to be wicked
glee. Finally, though, he pulled his chair over by hers to help
her deal with the barrage of questions.

"We thought perhaps we'd be married on New Year's
Day. That way Jenny will have time to get a little more
accustomed to the whole idea—" he glanced sideways at
her "—and the twins will still be on holiday so they can help
us celebrate—"

A burst of cheering from Joan and Geoffrey cut him short,
and then he turned to David and Anne, sitting close together.
"I know Jenny would rather not be married in the city, and
Cornwall is too far for all of you. Would it be possible for us
to be married here?"

He asked with unusual diffidence, and David and Anne
responded simultaneously. "Of course it would be possible.
It's an excellent idea."

"The great hall would be perfect for a wedding," Anne went on. "We'll have holiday decorations up and a fire going.... It'll be beautiful, and we'll all be thrilled to have a part in things."

The children wandered off, but the four adults sat on, planning together companionably. The thought occurred to Jenny that she had never seen Adam and Anne on such good terms; their meticulously polite treatment of each other had warmed, at least for the time being, into the easy behaviour of people who work together on something important to them both. Adam, too, treated Jenny with a sort of casual affection. She saw David and Anne take note of it and reminded herself with a sharp little pang that it must be just for show. Like herself, Adam would not want the others to guess the real nature of this marriage.

Momentarily distressed, Jenny felt her nerves tighten and her throat constrict, but soon the quiet murmur of the other three voices and the serenity of the old house itself seeped into her thoughts and she relaxed. In a brief moment of clarity she knew that she would go on with the marriage without regard to any sort of emotional caution, and she accepted the risks, hoping only that they might someday be justified. With an almost philosophical calm now, she was able to rejoin the conversation, glad that apparently none of the others had noticed her brief silence.

Some time later, David turned to her and asked smilingly, "When is the company going to lose its best secretary, Jenny?"

She acknowledged the compliment with an answering smile, but replied hesitantly, "Why, I don't know. I hadn't really thought about it."

"Well, I have," Adam cut in. "I have no intention of trying much longer to concentrate while you're there, my girl!"

She looked at him in surprise. Was this, too, just part of a show for David and Anne, or did he really prefer not to work with her for some reason? She was at a loss to think of a plausible explanation, but Anne unexpectedly agreed with Adam.

''I think Adam's right, Jenny. A girl who's planning a wedding shouldn't be running her fiancé's office at the same time. It's a bit much to do all at once!''

Fiancé. It was a word Jenny hadn't applied to Adam before, and for a moment she was distracted by it and looked at him with wide, curious blue eyes. He met her glance and held it, an expression in his own light gray eyes she couldn't read. She almost missed Anne's next words but was briefly recalled only by the sound of her name.

''We'd love to have you stay here as much as possible before the wedding, but you'll have a great deal to do before the New Year, Jenny. As well as ordering your wedding dress and having fittings, you'll probably want some new clothes for your trousseau, and you and Adam should think about a honeymoon.''

Her words drifted around Jenny, who was once again lost in her own thoughts. For the sake of having at least a legal tie to Adam, she had accepted the idea of marriage based on liking only, but sitting here among people who—dear as they were—were not her own family, she was swept by a sudden wave of longing for her own parents. She wanted desperately to talk to them, to share her wedding plans with them, confident that although their own loving marriage had been so different from the one she and Adam were about to embark on, they would understand her actions.

She wasn't aware of Adam's eyes on her, but lazily observant, they missed no detail of the small changes of expression flitting across her face. With quick accuracy he guessed the thoughts behind those changes and interrupted

Anne to speak with a perception that would have puzzled
Jenny had she not been too veiled by her own longing to
notice it.

"Jenny."

She turned her head slowly and saw that his face was
neither mocking nor unreadable, but only kind.

"Would you like to spend some time in Cornwall as soon
as you've trained someone else for your job and finished your
shopping in London? You could spend a few weeks there and
then come back here at Christmas." He glanced inquiringly
at David and Anne, and they nodded their agreement.

Cornwall. St. Just-in-Penwith and a small, gray stone
house that held most of her childhood memories. Dr.
Pennington, her oldest friend, with his kind advice and
support. Remembering Blair Graham's offer to move into his
aunt's house whenever she wanted to come home for a visit,
she said in a tremulous voice, "Yes, I'd like to do it that
way."

The remainder of the weekend had been happy, enlivened
by the children's nonsense, their parents' pleasure in the
engagement and Jenny's own anticipation of seeing Cornwall
again. Adam had continued to treat her with easy affection,
too, and she rashly let herself pretend it was real. When they
returned to London, Jenny was fortunate in having much less
trouble finding a good replacement than Miss Mayfair had
experienced. She quickly located a competent, motherly
woman who had decided to return to work because her
children were grown. She was soon familiar with the office
routine, and Jenny knew Adam and David would be well
looked after. Her own feelings about leaving the job were
mixed: she had always enjoyed working with David, and
working with Adam had been a bittersweet combination of
pleasure and pain—but one she would miss.

Still, leaving the job was a milestone on the way to

marrying Adam, and once she was finished at the offices of
Standish Publishing Company she enjoyed using the time to
shop for her wedding. No matter what the circumstances of
her marriage might be, Jenny found she wasn't immune to the
delights of wardrobe buying for this new stage in her life.
Without a qualm, she dug deeply into her savings,
determined that she would at least look the part of Adam's
wife, and brought back to her little room at the hostel pretty
suits and dinner dresses, with accessories to match; evening
gowns in jade silk and coral chiffon; a cobwebby shawl and
tiny gold lame evening bag; delicate sandals and handsome
walking shoes. She also abandoned a lifetime of practicality
and warmth in favor of delicate prettiness in her new
nightclothes, rejoicing in a froth of soft nylon and lace. When
she finished shopping, Jenny's tiny quarters bulged with soft,
bright fabrics that seemed an odd contrast to the spartan
nature of her room.

She also wrote letters. One was to Miss Mayfair to
announce her engagement—a careful letter that took her
several tries. The final result was a cheerful note that any
young woman soon to be married might have written, which
was just what Jenny had been trying for. She was too proud to
let even her elderly friend, who knew Adam so well, suspect
the real situation.

By return mail she received a letter from Kent that said,
with Miss Mayfair's usual kindly bluntness, that Adam was a
lucky man but Jenny herself had better watch her step in
dealing with a husband that complex; she wished them well,
however. Reading the letter, Jenny thought ruefully that Miss
Mayfair was more correct than she had any reason for being.
A man with Adam's mixture of sardonic playboy and diligent
executive, both coolly mocking and observantly kind, was
indeed complex, and Jenny would have to be doubly careful
because she loved where she was not loved in return.

Her other letters were to Blair Graham and Dr. Pennington, simply asking the former if her temporary repossession of the house could be managed and telling the latter when she expected to arrive. She didn't mention the reason for her visit to either man, feeling that Blair didn't really need to know and, for some reason, that she would prefer to tell Dr. Pennington her news in person rather than on paper.

Not surprisingly, she didn't hear from Dr. Pennington, an erratic correspondent, but Blair wrote back to say that his Aunt Susan had complained of feeling a bit neglected and would be delighted to take him in again for as long as Jenny wanted to stay in Cornwall.

Then suddenly everything she needed to do in London was done, and Adam arrived to pick up Jenny and all her possessions. Because of the nature of their marriage, they had decided to forgo a honeymoon and planned to return to Adam's house in Ennismore Mews after the wedding. Therefore, on the way to the train station, they made a brief stop in the mews to drop off the two new cases Jenny had bought for her trousseau.

Her thoughts finally returned to the present, and with a small tilt to the corners of her mouth, she picked up the newspapers Adam had bought her and dutifully began reading them. Surprisingly soon she was in Penzance, and there was Dr. Pennington, striding toward her. He met her with a bear hug, then hoisted her old cases and led her out to the familiar station wagon. Soon they had climbed the hill and were on the road west to St. Just, stopping twice for a few minutes at a time while Dr. Pennington checked briefly on a couple of patients. Before and after those stops he filled her in on the homely little doings of the village, then glanced across at her and said bluntly, ''Well, my dear, I'm delighted to see you but surprised you're back after only six months. That young publisher fellow didn't wear you to a frazzle with work or give you the sack, did he?''

Jenny took a deep breath and grinned to herself. Here it was.

"No," she answered clearly, "he asked me to marry him, and I accepted."

CHAPTER EIGHT

THAT EVENING Jenny and Dr. Pennington sat over coffee in the warm bright kitchen that Blair—and probably his Aunt Susan—had left immaculate, complete with a blue bowl of chrysanthemums on the table, for her arrival.

She had told her oldest friend almost everything, tracing her relationship with Adam from that first infuriating invitation to lunch through his proposal, to that second weekend with his family and her decision to come home for a few weeks before returning to Surrey for Christmas. The only thing she'd left out was Adam's qualification following his proposal. . . .

She had thought she would be able to tell Dr. Pennington the whole truth, pouring out her hopes and fears, her public happiness and her private confusion, but the words stuck in her throat. Perhaps her reticence was based on some sort of loyalty to Adam or on a reluctance to see worry come into the lined and much-loved face across from her; maybe it was just that she was no longer the child who had confidently taken every problem to a loving adult for a solution. At any rate, she kept her doubts to herself, sharing only her joys.

"Well, Jenny—" he put down his empty cup and refused her offer of another refill "—if I had been your Adam, I doubt I would have let you out of my sight, but I can't deny I'm pleased to have you here for as long as you two can stand to be parted. And maybe it's a good idea for you to get away from the city for a bit before your big day. Your cheeks have a thinness I don't much like, fashionable though it's said to be."

Thankful he couldn't read minds as well as he read faces, Jenny say him to the door and into the old coat that fit him like an aged-turtle's shell. He gave one of those thin cheeks an admonitory pat, ordered her to sleep well and left. She waved from the open doorway as his old car pulled away, then closed up the house for the night, on her face a lingering smile at his gruff concern.

The next three weeks were for Jenny a halcyon time. Adam wrote every three or four days, messages that were far from love letters but whose light ironic touch brought him clearly before her eyes. Taking her lead from him, she replied in much the same tone, detailing with her own gentle humor her activities and the small happenings of village life. She missed him badly at first, missed the daily contact and even the daily tension, but gradually she realized that this separation was giving her an interim of peace—the eye of the storm, she thought wryly, knowing how things would probably be when she and Adam were together again.

Cornwall was having an especially beautiful autumn, and Jenny reveled in its golden days. Often she rode with Dr. Pennington on his rounds, enjoying both the time spent in his company and the chance to drive through glowing afternoons in his wheezing old car. She also walked a great deal, and it was on her first evening back that she met Blair Graham as she was returning from a visit to her cliffside haunt. He had set up an easel in a small hollow, where the protected warmth felt like high summer, and was painting there, jacket off and sleeves rolled up along tanned forearms, when Jenny nearly stumbled into him. They recognized each other immediately, and after her breathless apology she thanked him for seeing that her house welcomed her.

"It was nothing. That's a very welcoming house," he said, brushing aside her thanks. He walked to where she had settled herself on the grass and lowered himself beside her.

She noticed that he moved far more easily than he had when she'd last seen him, and he read her thought.

"Yes," he said with a grin, "six months older and ten years younger! I feel like a new man and, better still, I paint like one. I hadn't realized how stale my technique had become until painting here gave me a new enthusiasm for my trade."

They talked comfortably together, as though they'd known each other for years, and he told her of the places he'd been painting. From there the talk wandered on to the abandoned tin-smelting towers, smugglers' caves on the Cornish coast and the mysterious standing stones of the prehistoric cromlechs and menhirs farther inland. Laughing as they tried to outdo each other, they peopled each place with its miners and free traders and dancing "merry maidens," inventing freely where their knowledge ran out. Both knew some of the famous stories of Cornish giants, too, and they exchanged tales, Jenny admitting frankly that in spite of her father's efforts to train her in the tradition of scholarly skepticism, she preferred, Cornish-born as she was, not to be caught out in the open at twilight.

Finally Blair climbed to his feet and extended a hand to Jenny. "If we're going to be indoors before the giants prowl tonight, we'll have to be on our way. Now that you've distracted me until the light is gone, you'll have to make amends tomorrow by taking me walking with you. Agreed?"

"Agreed. Shall I bring a picnic lunch for us both, while you bring your paints?"

"Readily agreed!" he said with a laugh.

The next day they walked all the way down to Land's End and stood on the steep cliffs watching the pounding waves of the Atlantic far below and the distant blue humps of the Scilly Isles. It was a day full of brilliant autumn sunshine, companionable talk, and long, equally companionable silences while Blair sketched and Jenny read the paperback book she had tucked into the pocket of her jacket. It was also the first of many such days, which both young people thoroughly enjoyed. Jenny found Blair undemanding company and a good friend, and he appeared to think of her the same way. When they talked, they spoke mostly of impersonal things or of similar tastes and different childhoods, neither speaking often of the greater complexities of adult life.

They traveled a great deal on foot and occasionally in Blair's small car when they wanted to go farther afield. They drove down to Marazion and at low tide crossed the causeway to climb St. Michael's Mount with its fairy-tale castle. In lovely St. Ives they wandered the winding streets, and Jenny visited the fascinating craft shops while Blair stopped in to see a friend from art-school days.

They also drove farther up the north coast of Cornwall to visit Tintagel, where Jenny, because of the old form of her name, always felt drawn. It was here that, according to Cornish legends, King Arthur had been born, and she chose to believe it. She and Blair crossed the narrow isthmus that linked the headland to the mainland and climbed to the romantic ruins of a castle that, although itself of a later period than that of Arthur, might have covered earlier traces of the great warrior chieftain. From a narrow sliver of beach along the mainland they also inspected Merlin's Cave, a tall crevice washed by occasional waves at both ends and floored with loose, silvery ovals of slate that made a musical sound when disturbed by feet. Time seemed to collapse around them, and both felt that the mighty magician was near.

Only once in all the time they spent together did any strain come between Jenny and Blair. It happened one afternoon on the cliffs when he was painting and she was staring dreamily out toward the sinking sun. As he worked, Blair mentioned over his shoulder that he was hoping to have a London show

of his paintings some time about midwinter and asked if
Jenny would be able to come and see what Cornwall had done
for him.

"Yes," Jenny answered unthinkingly. "Adam and I
should be settled by then, and I'd love to come."

Then she realized that the hand holding the paintbrush was
motionless, and she continued speaking with an awkward-
ness she didn't fully understand. "Blair, we've talked about
so many things, I didn't remember that wasn't one of them.
I'm marrying Adam Standish on New Year's Day."

The hand began to move again and, still with his back to
her, Blair said, "No, I didn't know, but there's no reason you
should have told me. I wish you every happiness."

Jenny was still oddly distressed, but Blair kept painting for
a while longer before he said, "I've lost my light. Shall we
go?"

After that he never again referred to a future outside
Cornwall but otherwise continued their friendship on the
same comfortable terms as before. Jenny accepted the tacit
limits also, but as it happened the long golden autumn finally
ended and days of continuous rain put a stop to their walks
together. Adam wrote suggesting that he come down to
Cornwall and drive her back to Repose for the Christmas
holidays, and Jenny agreed to be ready the following Saturday afternoon.

It was her last night in the beloved old house, and for a long
time she wandered quietly through it. Besides straightening
things up for Blair, so that the house would greet him again
when he came back, she was at the same time drawing
strength from the touch of her parents' furniture that she had
known since childhood. She felt very close to her parents just
then, and she breathed a tiny prayer that somehow, someday,
she and Adam would have the sort of marriage they had
shared.

She was packed and ready to go the next afternoon when Adam arrived. It was a cold wet day, and when he climbed rather wearily out of the car, she diffidently kissed his cool cheek and asked him into the kitchen for a cup of tea before he had to make the long trip back. He came in gladly, the gray eyes heavy lidded, and inside, he looked around the surprisingly big room at the heavy oak beams overhead, the old hutch full of blue and white china, the scrubbed table with its long benches, and the tiled hearth where a fire burned brightly to contradict the gloom outside. It was a happy room, full of the personalities of the man and woman who had furnished it and the child who had played and grown up there.

He accepted the steaming mug gratefully and cradled it in both hands, asking Jenny if he might see the rest of the house. Showing him around didn't take long, and soon they were back in the kitchen, where Adam lowered his long body into the embrace of the old rocking chair that stood by the hearth. He said nothing about the house except "Very nice, Guinevere," but he looked at her with an added understanding she did not see.

Just as he finished his tea and started to get reluctantly to his feet, there was a distinctive wheezing sound out front, and the doctor's old car stopped behind Adam's, its aged bulk a startling contrast with the smooth sleek lines of the Jaguar. In a moment the doctor himself arrived at the door on a gust of wind, his coat billowing around him.

"A quick detour on my rounds, Jenny," he said. "I wanted to catch you for a proper goodbye."

"I'm glad you did," she answered, taking his hand in one of hers and leading him in. "Now you can say hello to Adam and then goodbye to us both."

Adam had put down his mug and now came forward courteously, acknowledging Jenny's introduction and shaking hands with Dr. Pennington. For a moment they made polite conversation, agreeing that the weather left something to be desired. Each man studied the other intently. The doctor, of course, wanted to see what sort of man his beloved Jenny would be marrying; the reason for Adam's interest was less obvious.

At any rate, each seemed satisfied with what he saw. Then the doctor said, "I can't stay; I'm expected at old Mrs. Graham's to have a look at that arthritis of hers.

"Mr. Standish, you're getting a lovely wife; I've kept an eye on her since the day I delivered her, so I can attest to that. And you, Jenny my girl, see to it that your husband is as happy as your father was, and there'll be nothing else he could ask for." The tone was gruff, but he patted her cheek, less thin than it had been when she'd first returned home, and her eyes glistened brightly.

"Oh, please, as the bride's 'other father,' could you give me away?" she asked.

He cleared his throat, and that ingenous pink spread to the tips of his ears. "My dear, I'd be deeply honored." He seemed to have something else to say, but added only, "Write and tell me exactly when you want me to come, and I'll find myself a locum for the occasion.

"Now drive carefully through all this bad weather," he admonished, using the same tone to Adam that he used to Jenny and causing Adam to grin at her resulting discomfiture.

Then he turned back at the door. "Jenny, I almost forgot. Blair Graham called me at my office this morning and asked me to say his goodbyes for him. I'll be dropping by his Aunt Susan's, and I'll leave word for him that you got safely on your way."

Adam arched a dark eyebrow but said nothing, and Jenny, somewhat flustered, asked the doctor to wish Blair well. A final wave, and her old friend sprinted with surprising speed through the rain to his car and was gone.

Jenny watched until the car was out of sight, then turned back into the kitchen. Adam was at the sink, just putting down the towel he had used to dry his mug, and amusement at the domesticated picture he presented changed the lump in Jenny's throat to a burble of laughter.

"And what, may I ask, is so funny?" he inquired with mock severity. "Didn't you think I knew how to wash and dry a mug?"

"No!" Jenny chuckled. "It's a side of you I haven't seen before."

"You're likely to see quite a few more of those, my girl," he answered as he walked over to retrieve his coat from the rocking chair. There was a gleam in his eye that puzzled her. He didn't give her time to wonder about it, or time to say protracted goodbyes to the house, either, for that matter, but expertly banked the fire on the hearth and swept her neatly into her coat and then into the car. He dropped her cases in the trunk, slid into the driver's seat, and they pulled away into the misty gray afternoon.

For the first hour or so they made desultory conversation, Jenny asking about the London office and Adam answering with tales—apocryphal, she was certain—of the way things had fallen apart without her expert hand to guide them. Still, even though she didn't believe a word he said, it was heartwarming that he should bother with such flattery.

As the early darkness closed in around them, there were longer silences in the green car. Adam broke one of them to say thoughtfully, "I like your Dr. Pennington, Jenny. I think I would have liked your parents, too, judging by their friend, their house and of course their daughter."

Jenny murmured a reply, and silence took over again. Eventually, lulled by the purr of the engine, she dozed off, and as he had done before, Adam cradled her limp, young body against him. With a wry smile into the darkness, he acknowledged to himself that he was getting rather good at watching over Jenny while she slept. Then he concentrated on his driving.

They arrived at Repose hours later, to be met by Anne, who had waited up. All three of them slept late into the next morning.

CHAPTER NINE

JENNY SOON DISCOVERED that Anne believed Christmas in an Elizabethan house should be celebrated with as much of the pageantry of an Elizabethan holiday as possible. Delighted, Jenny flung herself into the preparation with as much abandonment as the children.

During the next few days she and the twins went outside to gather holly, mistletoe and ivy. Adding dried rosemary for its fragrance, they strung garlands around the great hall, the lovely shallow staircase, the long gallery upstairs, and everywhere else they could reach.

Anne baked constantly in her big kitchen, with whatever help she could recruit in passing from the children and Jenny. With—or perhaps in spite of—their help she produced cakes, rectangular plum puddings, pies, mince tarts and breads that filled the house with delectable smells. She did, however, draw the line at a boar's-head feast, saying that she knew her limitations, and one of them was serving a meal that still looked like the animal it came from. The twins pleaded with her, trying to break down her resistance by saying how lovely the pig's head would look on a large platter, surrounded by bay leaves and rosemary and covered with a sweet sauce, a bright red apple in its mouth, but Anne was laughingly adamant, so they reluctantly settled for a roast goose stuffed with onions and apples.

Another occasion where tradition was bent somewhat was over the question of a Christmas tree. Like the roast goose, it was more Victorian than Elizabethan, but Anne's weak suggestion that they might do without one that year in the interests of historical accuracy brought such a howl of protest from the children that she quickly let herself be overruled.

David and Adam were commissioned to find a tree, and they fulfilled their commission nobly. The fir they brought in and placed in front of the wide windows of the hall, well away from the heat of the hearth, must have been at least twelve feet tall, its branches forming an elegant sweeping cone, like the heavy skirts of some great lady.

As soon as the tree was set up, the men went out again to retrieve the Yule log they'd found to burn in the huge fireplace of the great hall. With grunting ceremony they carried in the enormous oak root, stripped of its bark, and laid it ready to be lit on Christmas eve with a brand from the previous year's log.

Throughout all this, the house was filled with rustling paper and whispered consultations in which Jenny, too, had a part as the twins asked her advice about presents for their mother and father and Adam. Actually, she was also having her own trouble deciding what to give Adam, although she had ordered several things from London for other members of the family and had gratefully accepted David's offer one day of a lift into Guildford for shopping.

She had a lovely gossamerlike stole for Anne; for Teddy a stuffed toy giraffe to replace the lamb, by then little more than a chewed-up remnant; a tin for David of the special tobacco Anne said he liked to smoke; and for the twins she had ordered the costumes they would wear for the wedding, again with Anne's advice. But Adam was still a problem, and there, of course, Anne was no help, even though she and Adam seemed to have made a tacit truce.

Finally, in sheer desperation, Jenny bought Adam a very beautiful leather-bound edition of Elizabeth Barrett Browning's love poems, *Sonnets from the Portuguese*, then alternated between a gnawing suspicion that to give it to him would reveal far too much of her feelings and a defeated certainty that to return it would leave her without any gift for him at all. In the end she wrapped it and hid it from sight for as long as possible, refusing to think about the problem anymore.

Christmas eve arrived at last, and suddenly all the other preparations were finished. Nearly explosive with excitement, the children decorated the lower branches of the Christmas tree—Teddy gravely placing his two ornaments on the same branch, where they were invisible to anyone who stood taller than he—while the adults used their longer reach and a stepladder on the upper branches.

When it was finished and properly admired, they all went off to their secret gift troves and returned carrying rustling armloads of mysterious bundles, which were then placed under the glittering fir tree. Jenny tucked Adam's gift as far in under the heap as she could manage, then kept a laughing watch until the children were reluctantly convinced not to shake, poke or rattle the packages that bore their names.

The Yule log was ceremoniously lit, and in the tradition of ancient mummers the children presented their version of the old play *St. George and the Dragon*. Some discussion had arisen out of Geoffrey's desire to be both the saint and the dragon, but he finally chose the saint and played him in fine heroic style, slaying Joan—the dragon—with grand gestures. As the doctor who is supposed to revive the dragon, Teddy was enchanting, poking and tugging Joan while he urged, "Get up, dragon, do!"

After that excitement, everyone gathered in front of the fire and for a time played a boisterous game in which each player named a nonsensical tongue-twisting gift, and then repeated in reverse order all those already named by the other players.

The game done—because the participants finally admitted

their minds and tongues were defeated—the family and Jenny gathered around David, who read the Christmas story beautifully. Then Anne disappeared for a few minutes, coming back diffidently with a lovely little minstrel's harp. Seeing Adam's expression of surprise, she said gently, "I do play occasionally," and he had the grace to look embarrassed.

They cleared a space around her chair, and Anne sat down with the harp cradled in her lap. In a clear, sweet contralto she led them through a medley of Christmas carols. Teddy climbed confidingly into Jenny's arms, and Adam pulled his chair close to hers and sang in a pleasant baritone with his arm resting lightly over her shoulders. Jenny gave herself up to the joys of the moment.

Finally, Anne called a halt, seeing that Teddy was soundly asleep in Jenny's lap and the twins were fighting a losing battle against their yawns; even the men didn't look especially alert, although Jenny would have been content to stay just as she was for hours yet. Nevertheless, Anne put her harp aside, and she and David herded the blinking twins off to bed while Jenny carried a sleeping Teddy upstairs to his nursery, Adam following in their wake.

Up in the little boy's cozy room, she gently undressed him and inserted him into his flannel-footed pajamas, while Adam watched quietly from the dim doorway. Teddy didn't awake even as she deposited him in his crib, and brushing Teddy's fine baby hair off his forehead, she kissed him lightly and walked to the door. Adam looked at her in the half light from the long gallery.

"You do that as though you'd had years of practice," he murmured quizzically.

"Well, I haven't," she whispered back, "but it seems easy."

He said nothing more about it, only setting Teddy's door

ajar and taking her arm to usher her downstairs again for a quick good night to David and Anne.

They found the other two sitting side by side on an old wooden settle near the glowing Yule log and busily stuffing apples, candy and small toys into the childrens' stockings. They didn't stop as Adam and Jenny came down the stairs, but only looked up with weary smiles.

"The trouble," Anne said in a thread of a voice, "is that after bundling those two hooligans into bed, I don't have enough strength left to do the same for myself."

She smiled at David. "After I finish playing Santa Claus, you may just have to leave me here all night."

He levered himself slowly to his feet, placed the now bulging stockings in front of the tree and reached down to haul his wife up beside him. "Not a chance," he grinned, "and have you snooping through the packages as soon as you got a second wind?"

"Unjust!" she accused, turning to Jenny. "You see how he treats me?" she appealed, before David put an arm around her waist and piloted her toward the stairs. Over her shoulder she called back, "An early good night, then. The children will undoubtedly see to it that we have a very early good morning!"

Laughing together, Jenny and Adam followed them up the stairs, and when they reached Jenny's door Adam brushed the tip of her nose with a light kiss and left her. She shut the door softly, then peeled off her clothes and let them drop into an inelegant pile, before falling gratefully into bed.

Anne was right. It was barely light outside when the twins plopped Teddy onto Jenny's bed to wake her, while they themselves danced around the room whooping, "Jenny, wake up! It snowed, Jenny!"

True enough. Jenny opened her eyes to see her room filled with the cold white light that reflects off fresh snow—

the perfect finishing touch to their old-fashioned Christmas.

The twins were optimistic that she wouldn't shut her eyes again once she'd seen the marvelous snow; so they grabbed the warm bundle that was Teddy off her bed and with a shout of ''Merry Christmas!'' bolted out the door to rouse the rest of the household. In fact it was touch and go for a minute as Jenny sleepily weighed the pleasures of warm covers against the thoughts of a chill Christmas morning; then, with a chuckle, she realized that if she didn't get out of bed the twins would probably come back and roll her out.

Throwing back the covers with a shiver, she looked longingly for a moment at the fire laid ready on her hearth, then decided it would take too long to heat the room, anyway. Instead, she hurried into a long plaid skirt and a high-necked black sweater, thrusting her legs into warm tights and her feet into comfortable old loafers. A quick wash in the adjoining bathroom, a few flicks of a brush through her silky hair, which was then held off her forehead with a tortoiseshell clip, a touch of coral lipstick, and she was ready—almost as fast as the children could have wished.

As she stepped out into the long hall, they were on their way to check on her; they dragged her to the stairs just as Anne and David appeared, also warmly dressed and sleepy eyed but laughingly resigned. Adam must have offered the children the most resistance, because he was the last to present himself, but soon he, too, came into sight—looking devastatingly handsome, Jenny thought, in an old green jersey and dark green slacks.

At last everyone was assembled at the top of the steps, where the children danced impatiently and nearly flew downstairs the instant Anne allowed them. They pounced joyously on their stockings, while the adults came down the stairs with rather more decorum. When the stockings had been emptied and the Yule log stirred into a fresh blaze, they seated themselves comfortably on the scattered chairs and sofas, and David began handing out the gaily wrapped parcels, calling out each recipient's name as he read the tag.

Jenny spent much of her time watching the children. While Anne helped Teddy open his presents, the twins managed for themselves with eager efficiency. They were excited by a variety of both practical and entertaining presents from their parents, Adam and also Anne's great-aunt in Scotland, a crusty old lady who, inevitably, year after year sent mohair sweaters in the belief that children could never be *too* warm. But it was Jenny's long, flat boxes that produced the most delight.

True to her promise that they would be in the wedding, she had bought for the twins the outfits they would wear, Joan as her one attendant and Geoffrey as her usher. A look of rapture on her face, Joan withdrew from the box her first long dress. It was a rich green velvet in a sort of medieval cut with a high waistline, square neck and long, flowing sleeves. For Geoffrey, Jenny had wisely resisted the temptation to dress him in a medieval page boy's tights and tunic and had purchased a green velvet suit, which somehow managed to avoid making him look like Little Lord Fauntleroy.

Unself-consciously stripping off their outer clothes right where they stood, the twins tried on their velvet outfits immediately. Soon, looking anxiously for approval, they stood in front of their parents, and Adam and Jenny. They received it at once, as the adults told them how elegant they looked. In fact, in their eager innocence, they seemed the embodiment of Christmases past celebrated in the old house.

Jenny's eyes misted for a moment as she looked at them, and she could only nod her approval before Anne brought things back to earth by warning the twins that they should get back into their ordinary clothes before anything became torn or stained. They stripped again and soon were just the freckle-faced twins again, no longer visitors from Christ-mases of long ago.

Jenny's own gifts included potholders from Joan and a doorstop from Geoffrey, both "for your own house"; a soft, warm sweater that Anne had knitted herself and a beautiful, old-fashioned gold bracelet from David. Opening that box, Jenny lifted delighted eyes to him.

She had called Anne by her first name from the beginning and had long since slipped into thinking of her husband as David; now she called him that aloud. "It's lovely. Oh, David, thank you so much!" Then she heard her words and blushed, trying to frame an apology.

Before she could do so, David forestalled her by saying gruffly, "About time you figured out what my name was, young woman. I was getting tired of hearing that Mr. Standish business when you're not even working for the company anymore."

Then he nodded at the worn, leather box in Jenny's hand. "That belonged to my grandmother, who died when I was a little boy. I remember her, though, and I want you to have her bracelet, Jennifer; she would have approved, too, I think."

Unable to thank him in words, Jenny stood up and, still holding the box, walked over to him and reached up to kiss his cheek. He gave her a one-armed hug and said softly, "Welcome to the family, Jenny."

The last present Jenny opened was a small box from Adam. She held it for a minute, wondering what he had thought to give a woman he was marrying out of friendship rather than love. Then she slipped the little box out of its silver paper and opened it.

Inside was an engagement ring, the loveliest Jenny had ever seen, and she uttered a soft gasp at the sight of it. On a plain gold band was a perfect opal, its graceful oval shape surrounded by small, brilliant sapphires. She looked up to see

Adam watching her from his chair across the hearth. Standing, he crossed to her side and took the ring to slip it on her finger. It fit perfectly, gleaming softly on her hand.

"It suits you, Guinevere," he said, and she tore her eyes away from the lovely ring to look up at him in bewilderment. This wasn't the sort of present a man gave the "friend" he was marrying, but rather the sort he would give the bride he adored.

"Adam, it's beautiful," she stammered, "but you needn't have. . . . It must have been terribly expensive. . . ."

She trailed off because on his face was the hard mocking expression she knew well but had seen rarely the past couple of weeks.

"Oh, don't worry, Jennifer—" his words were not loud enough to reach the ears of any of the others "—it's expected of your eager fiancé. And what's a little money when everyone knows it paves the way to a woman's heart?" And with that he walked away, hands in his pockets, leaving her frozen in her chair by the warm fire.

At that moment the twins caught sight of the hand that she still held motionless in front of her and rushed over to see Adam's gift. "Oooh, Jenny," Joan breathed, "isn't it beautiful!"

More slowly Anne and David also approached, adding their enthusiasm to the twins', and somehow Jenny managed to answer in the excited tones of a girl who has just received a gift from the man who loves her. She was devoutly thankful when the others drifted away at last and she was alone for a moment to cope with the pain in her heart.

She had been living in a fool's paradise, letting herself dream that because Adam had been treating her with casual kindliness in front of his family his feelings for her must be warming into love. The truth she had refused to accept was that he didn't love her now any more than he had when he proposed that they marry so she could have a home of her own and he could escape the social whirl of London. Their marriage would be only one of mutual convenience, and he would feel the same as he did now about her on their wedding day and even ten years hence. He had chosen to remind her of their circumstances rather brutally, but perhaps she should be grateful that he had shattered her illusions before she completely lost touch with reality.

The ring at which she had been so blindly staring glowed up at her, and Jenny wrenched her eyes away and saw Adam on the far side of the room by the Christmas tree. As she watched, he bent and picked up her present to him, somehow overlooked by David as he handed out gifts. Partly turned away from her, Adam opened the package, then stood for a long moment with the beautiful edition of love poems lying in his hands.

Slowly he began to turn toward her, and Jenny, panic-stricken, rose from her chair. If only she had thought to snatch that package from under the tree a minute ago! She could have said she'd ordered him a present from London that hadn't arrived in time. Anything to avoid having her declaration of love follow his declaration of indifference!

Mercifully, Anne called from the end of the hall just then. "Jenny, while I stir things in the kitchen, would you round up the children and chase them into clothes that are fit to be seen at church?"

"Yes, of course," she called back and bolted up the stairs, leaving Adam to gaze after her, a peculiar expression on his face.

All through Christmas services in the village church, Jenny was distracted, removed from the rejoicing around her and afterward only half-aware of shaking hands with the vicar who had agreed to perform her marriage ceremony in a week's time. Over and over her thoughts ran in the same circle.

Marriage to Adam, living every day with a man she adored and having to accept his casual attitude to her, would be uncomfortable at best and agonizing at worst. But at the same time the thought of living the rest of her life without him, without his impossible blend of sharp mockery and thoughtful kindness, made her hands clench and her breath come raggedly. What sort of choice did she have, really, between the tensions of life with Adam and the utter barrenness of life without him?

As they sat in the back of Adam's car on the way home from church, Teddy bounced onto her lap. As her arms closed automatically around him she wondered with a fresh pang if she could give up Adam's family any more easily than she could give up Adam himself. She had grown to love them all so dearly.

Dinner was a festive meal, preceded by a wassail bowl with bits of toast and nuts floating on top of the steaming punch. Anne's roast goose was delicious, but Jenny barely tasted it. Nor did she enjoy the snowball fight the twins insisted on after dinner as a way to "settle" stomachs or the building of an absurd snowman among the topiary of the formal garden. She was hardly aware of the friends and neighbors who dropped in during the afternoon and responded politely but absentmindedly to their good wishes. Only when Adam came near her did she chatter brightly before finding the first excuse to move away.

She helped Anne fix a light supper that was left nearly untouched, so full was everyone from the earlier feast and afternoon snacking, then together they put to bed children too tired for anything but half-hearted protests. That done, Jenny said good night to Anne upstairs in the long gallery. "Anne, thank you for my present and for making me part of your family celebration. You've made me feel as if I've come home.''

''We hope you'll always feel that way about coming here, love. Now go to bed; you look done in. I'll say good night to David for you and send Adam up to see you.''

And with a quick hug she ran lightly down the stairs before Jenny could think of any plausible excuse why Adam should not come up to say good night. She was still standing where Anne had left her when Adam reached the top of the stairs only a minute later. With the lean grace that was one of the many things she loved about him, he walked toward her, took her arm in his and led her to the door of her room. There he stopped and released her arm so that he could turn her to face him.

''You look all eyes, Guinevere,'' he said, and the tired blue eyes filled at the sound of the name only he and her father had called her. At that he took her in his arms and cradled her head against his shoulder, in the same way he might have comforted one of the twins.

''Oh, you poor thing. I'm sorry to have spoiled your Christmas and blighted your pleasure in a gift I wanted you to enjoy.'' He raised the hand wearing his ring, which she tried to ignore all day, pressed a gentle kiss into its palm, then sighed, ''I can't seem to remember who you are.''

To Jenny the words held a rather disturbing note, but pressed against Adam's chest so that she could feel the soft fabric of his jersey warmed by his skin and hear the steady beat of his heart, she was too contented to move and ask what he meant. He did not volunteer any explanation, only stroking her hair with a comforting hand. All too soon he held her away from him again and, giving her a brief, warm kiss on the lips, turned her toward her room and gave her a little push. ''Now off with you, my girl, and sleep well.'' Obediently she went into her room and in a few minutes was soundly and dreamlessly asleep.

CHAPTER TEN

TO THE CHILDREN'S DELIGHT the river was frozen on Boxing Day. They held a skating party, but after that almost everyone's time was filled with wedding preparations.

Adam and his father discreetly made themselves scarce, Adam even going to the city a couple of times. The twins, meanwhile, were charged with keeping the holiday decorations fresh, replacing them with new greens when necessary, a responsibility they took very seriously. Jenny herself occasionally helped Anne with the baking, but more often she was ousted good-naturedly from the kitchen and told to worry about her own preparations.

Actually, though, there were comparatively few of those. She had written to Dr. Pennington, asking him to come up to Repose the morning of the wedding and extending Anne's invitation for him to stay at the house that night. She wondered about Blair Graham, too, knowing his name was on the list of people to whom Anne had sent invitations, but Jenny guessed he wouldn't come; he would probably be far too busy preparing for his London show.

The twins watched with excited curiosity as Jenny opened the wedding presents that began to pour in to the Standish house from country friends and city associates. She wrote graceful thank-you letters to acknowledge gifts ranging from practical blankets to exquisite crystal.

Four days before the wedding, Jenny's gown, which she had had fitted before leaving London, arrived in a huge white box. She immediately carried it off to her room, refusing in spite of all their pleas to let the twins or even Anne see it. She told them it was to be a surprise and extracted from the twins a reluctant promise that they wouldn't try to peek when she was out of her room.

Then suddenly it was Jenny's wedding day, crisp and beautiful, and the small group of guests that Anne had invited had no trouble driving in for the ceremony. Dr. Pennington had arrived safely, too, on a wave of hearty greetings, bringing word from Blair that he was painting madly but wished them all the best; he was made to feel at home by the family the same way Jenny had been.

Certainly the ceremony was a family affair. At the front door the guests were greeted by Geoffrey, resplendent in his green velvet, and ushered to chairs, benches and settles in front of the long windows of the lovely, candlelit great hall. Meanwhile, Anne, who wore a gown of delicate rose satin, played her harp softly. When everyone had been seated, Adam took his place near the hearth where the Yule log still burned, David beside him as best man. Both wore jackets of dark green velvet with ruffled shirts above the satin-striped pants of their formal wear; Jenny had requested them to wear something traditional, for reasons she wouldn't explain.

At last Anne's music changed, and everyone stood to look at the long, shallow staircase. Down it, solemn in her long dress, its rich green shining against the warm oak paneling around her, came a strangely dignified Joan; behind her, Jenny walked beside her oldest friend, her hand tucked securely in the crook of his arm.

And there was the dress Jenny had been so secretive about, the dress for which she had willingly drained her savings account. For this unusual wedding she had chosen to wear an unusual gown, one that suited the lovely Elizabethan house in which the ceremony was held. Made of heavy white satin that gleamed with threads of fine silver embroidery, it had a tight-fitted bodice that came to a point at her waist, then spread into a very wide full skirt that brushed the floor. The sleeves were also long and full, and over them were loosely fastened panels of white satin that fell in points below her wrists. Out of the graceful square neckline rose a dainty ruff that stood up around the back of her neck, its fine white lace framing her face. She wore no veil, only a white rose tucked into the shining dark hair she had piled on top of her head; more white roses made up the bouquet she carried in her left hand.

Like a beautiful Renaissance portrait come to life, she walked noiselessly down the stairs and came to stand beside Adam, whose eyes burned again with that small flame. Then, her expression serene, all the doubting voices in her mind resolutely silenced, she married Adam Standish.

At the end of a wedding reception that had been enlivened by the antics of the twins, all their unnatural solemnity forgotton, Jenny stood on the stairs and tossed her bouquet neatly into Joan's hands—much to the little girl's delight— then went to her room, where Anne helped her into the trim, blue wool suit she had bought for the occasion.

When she was ready to go, Anne hugged her and whispered, ''Jenny, I'm so glad for you . . . and for Adam. Forget what I said about him in the garden that day; I'm sure it isn't true anymore. And be happy—we all want that so much.''

Downstairs again there were more farewells, including hugs from Dr. Pennington and Miss Mayfair and one of Teddy's special kisses. But soon they were on their way, Adam's Jaguar moving through a rain of confetti, then down the long driveway and onto the road for London and Adam's house in the mews.

Smiling still, Jenny settled back into the deep, leather upholstery and turned her head to watch Adam's profile as he drove. He let her look her fill and then glanced briefly at her, one tilted eyebrow raised. "Satisfied, Mrs. Standish?" he asked in gentle mockery.

She nodded, and he continued, "My shoulder is available if you'd like to sleep; we have some distance to go, of course, and it has been a rather full day." He grinned at the understatement, then saw her hesitation. "You've done it before, Jenny, only you were too soundly asleep to know! It's all right; you won't interfere with my driving, and I've grown used to your habit of dropping off!"

Jenny smiled guiltily, but in fact as she relaxed into the motion of the car she was—as usual—beginning to feel somewhat sleepy. Perhaps, too, the emotional turmoil of the past week was taking its toll. At any rate, happily persuaded she'd be no trouble to Adam, she slipped over and rested her head on his shoulder. She rubbed her face against the soft cashmere of his jacket and breathed in a scent compounded of soap and shaving lotion and warm skin, and in a few minutes she was fast asleep.

She slept soundly all the way to London, and even when Adam drove into Ennismore Mews and parked the Jaguar Jenny didn't awake immediately. For a moment after he switched off the engine, Adam simply sat motionless in the dim light that entered the car from the house, then he turned his head so that his cheek brushed Jenny's silky hair. He caught his breath, and when he finally exhaled, soft tendrils stirred along her temple and she murmured sleepily. He left a brief kiss where his breath had been and turned away again with an abrupt movement.

"Wake up, Jenny; we're home," he said briskly, sliding out of the car as she sat up. A few moments later he helped her from the car and led her to the front door, which was promptly opened by Timothy Brown. Inside, Adam introduced his new wife to both Timothy and Mrs. Brown, who had bustled in from the kitchen, and Jenny, gathering her wits, acknowledged their good wishes with instinctive charm. While Timothy took their coats, Adam briefly told the Browns about the wedding and their trip from Repose, while Jenny gazed around at the small foyer with its beautiful black and white parquet floor. It was hard to believe that she had come here as Adam's wife and that the wedding ceremony earlier had not been just a part of her dreams in the car.

As she thought, a series of expressions flitted across Jenny's face. Mrs. Brown noted them, watching with unobtrusive kindliness, and when Adam had finished, she said, "All worn out from it your wife is, and no wonder, with the way weddings are. Shall I bring a light supper for you both upstairs?"

With a glance at Jenny, who nodded gratefully, Adam agreed. Then he stepped closer to her and offered her his arm with a gallant gesture. "May I escort you upstairs, my lady? You may survey the rest of your new kingdom tomorrow at your leisure."

Responding to his tone, Jenny gracefully took the arm he presented and returned, "Thank you, kind sir. I would be delighted to accept your offer." And while Timothy and his wife smiled from below, the newlyweds swept up the stairs.

At the top of the staircase, Adam led Jenny to a doorway where he released her hand. "Go in and get acquainted, Jenny, while the Browns and I see to the luggage and decide precisely what's to be included in that light supper." With a smile he clicked his heels and sketched the satiric suggestion of a bow, then vanished back down the stairway while Jenny gazed wistfully after him for a moment. Then she opened the door in front of her.

The room she entered was lovely, newly decorated for Jenny on Adam's instructions. A fine, soft Oriental rug in muted shades of aqua, rose and ivory covered most of the polished wood floor, and walls and bedspread echoed the same delicate aqua. The canopy over the wide bed and the long drapes were ivory, as was the day bed piled with rose cushions and drawn up beside a fireplace where a cheerful little fire burned. A graceful eighteenth-century desk and a few small chairs completed the furnishings, and doors opened into a large dressing room and a luxuriously appointed bathroom.

Jenny admired the bathroom for a moment, then walked over to splash her face at the cool marble basin and enjoy the gentle touch of a soft turquoise towel laid out ready for use. A knock at the outer door announced Timothy with the cases Jenny had brought up from Repose, and when he had gone she spent some time contentedly arranging the rest of her things in the drawers and cupboards of the ample dressing room where Mrs. Brown had already unpacked her trousseau.

She was just finishing when Adam's voice announced from the bedroom that supper had arrived, and she hurried eagerly from the dressing room to find him setting a large tray on the desk. When she offered to help, though, he refused to let her. "Oh no, you don't, Mrs. Standish," he said, with a stern lowering of eyebrows. "You establish yourself on that day bed like a lady of leisure and I shall serve you your first meal as mistress of this household."

Laughing, Jenny retreated and settled herself decorously on the lounge while Adam brought a low table from another room and covered it with a small white cloth. That done, he spread their supper on it, revealing to Jenny's suddenly interested eyes a delicate crab soufflé, crisp salad, cheese and biscuits and an iced bottle of champagne. Then, with Jenny watching and silently rejoicing in each of her husband's deft movements, he uncorked the champagne, poured two glasses and handed one to her.

He gave Jenny a long look, from which teasing mockery had vanished, then said simply, "A toast to a lovely bride, Guinevere." Then he drank, turning away a moment later to stir the fire.

His words echoed around Jenny, and suddenly her breathing was constricted. She was indeed a bride. The beautiful ceremony at Repose that afternoon had been no dream, and the man whose back was to her in this softly shadowed bedroom was her husband. With a tiny gasp she took a convulsive sip of her champagne . . . and choked.

Adam was at her side immediately, and when the coughing stopped he gave her his handkerchief to mop her streaming eyes. While she made herself presentable again, he went around to the far side of the table and settled his long length on the rug, feet toward the fire's warmth, weight propped negligently on one elbow. Then he looked up at Jenny, now composed, and said sweetly, "You'll have to do better than that for conversation, my girl," and ducked the pillow that Jenny, in laughing indignation, hurled at his head.

Adam retrieved her rose-colored weapon and calmly wedged it under his elbow, settling himself as comfortably as a banqueting Roman, then proceeded to make their supper together so merry that the realization that had so startled Jenny a few minutes earlier slipped quietly to the back of her mind. They ate all of Mrs. Brown's delicious supper, and if Jenny drank a bit too much champagne she didn't care, only aware that she was warm and gay, relaxed and very happy.

It was extremely late when the last of their meal was gone, and a companionable silence fell between them. Finally Adam stood up to put another log on the fire and turned to Jenny, who lay dreamily against her remaining cushions, gazing into the flames. Feeling his glance, she lifted her eyes to him and he looked down at her, his face, turned from the firelight, barely visible.

"I'll leave you now, Jenny," he said quietly. "I can save Mrs. Brown a bit of effort in the morning if I return the remains of our feast to her kitchen tonight." And bending, he brushed a kiss across her cheek and then gathered up their dishes. In a moment he was gone.

For a little while after the door closed softly after him, Jenny lay where she was, her vision filled with the dancing flames. At last she roused herself and made her way into the glamorous bathroom, where a hot, lilac-scented bath lulled her further. Afterward, she wrapped herself in a huge fluffy towel and went into the dressing room to burrow in the drawer where Mrs. Brown had put the riot of filmy nightwear Jenny had bought for her trousseau.

She was hunting for one particular purchase, made late one afternoon in a mood of reckless daring, and she soon found it. A minute later, the towel lay abandoned, and Jenny was looking in the full-length mirror, seeing herself in a nightgown that barely deserved the title since it was nearly invisible. There was a matching negligee, somewhat more modest and trimmed with a drift of soft feathers at throat and wrists; Jenny, pink cheeked, put it on with more haste than grace. She did not, however, consider changing nightgowns, and once the negligee's silky ribbons were tied she tilted her chin at the mirror with a sort of gamine defiance, curtsied to her reflection, murmuring, "Good night, Mrs. Standish," and returned to the bedroom.

The wide bed had been turned down, but Adam was nowhere to be seen, and she hesitated in the middle of the room. The elegant little clock on the desk said half-past two; surely Adam would be back any minute. Deciding at last that she'd prefer to wait for him by the fire, Jenny returned to the day bed and settled gracefully among the soft rose cusions.

In a way it was pleasant to have a little while to think before Adam returned and made her his wife in every sense of the word. Alone now she had time to think about the girl she had been and dream of the woman she would be. She thought of her parents, without the old stab of grief, and understood more clearly than ever before what they had meant to each other. Hearing in her mind the timeless promises she and Adam had made that day, she knew her parents had kept those same promises and vowed again to keep them herself.

Gazing into the embers at the fire's enchanted heart, Jenny lost herself in its spell and looked into the future, down a long sunlit avenue of years with Adam, years when all barriers between them would have crumbled. Her earlier feeling of panic banished, she dreamed on in the firelight, waiting tranquilly now for Adam to return and their married life to begin. And when he came to her, much later, she was asleep.

He opened the door quietly, still fully dressed and with an expression on his face that seemed oddly haggard for a newly wedded man. Seeing that Jenny was not in bed, he crossed to the fireside where she had fallen asleep and stood looking down at her in the last faint glow from the embers.

For a few silent moments he gazed at his wife, noting the fan of lashes that lay on her cheek, the soft movements of her breathing, and the unconscious grace of her relaxed body. Then his lips tightened, and with impersonal efficiency, he undid the ribbons Jenny had tied earlier and slipped her gently out of the feathery nonsense of her negligee. Laying it aside, he hesitated an instant before gathering Jenny and her remaining scrap of nylon into careful arms. At the warmth of his touch, she stirred slightly but didn't awake, and still with a taut look on his face, Adam carried her to the comfortable bed and slid her as easily as a child beneath the soft bedclothes.

As he did so, Jenny mumbled something indistinct, and he bent to hear it. She said nothing more, but for a long time Adam stayed where he was, leaning over her. Finally, with a sigh he brushed the tumbled hair away from her face and kissed her gently; then he left the bedroom, shutting the door with a quiet little click behind him. In a few minutes muffled sounds in the next room indicated that he, too, was going to bed for the few remaining hours of the night.

IN THE MORNING Jenny awoke alone. She awoke slowly, stretching luxuriously, conscious at first only of a feeling of rest and refreshment. Then as she became more alert, she recognized the aqua room around her. The wedding came back to her in a glad rush, but confusion followed immediately. She remembered her firelit supper with Adam; she remembered waiting for him later by the fire in her daring nightwear—Jenny looked down at herself, realizing that her concealing negligee was gone and that she did not remember taking it off or coming to bed. Her cheeks reddened as she realized Adam must have put her to bed. But where was he now?

Almost as if her thought had been an incantation, he appeared, following a brief tap at the door. He had a tray in one hand, but he crossed the room to pull open the long curtains and let in a flood of winter sunlight before returning to Jenny and placing the tray across her lap. He tossed her a brief smile, then said mockingly, "Breakfast is served, madam. I trust you slept well, Mrs. Standish?"

"Yes, thank you," she murmured automatically, but her thoughts were racing. She had slept very well indeed; she had also slept alone—alone on her wedding night.

She had known the previous day when she'd spoken her vows at Repose that Adam didn't love her, but when he proposed a friendly marriage she had assumed that in other respects it would be a normal one. Under her lashes she swept a furtive look around the room. There was no trace of Adam in it; she realized now that it was a completely feminine room, without any indications that he had been there last night or that he ever intended being there on any future night.

A small pain stung her heart. She would be doing without the love of a normal marriage; must she do without the closeness, too? She toyed with the toast Adam had brought and asked with difficulty, "And you . . . did you sleep well?"

At his impassive nod, she stumbled on. "Adam, where did you sleep?"

He left the small chair by her bed and walked toward the fireplace, bending to stir the ashes and lay on fresh kindling. Without looking back at her, he answered, "In my own room next door, of course."

Too hurt for maidenly reticence, Jenny blurted, "But I'm your wife!"

At that he did face her again, and the distance between them might have been light-years. "Not in the usual sense of the word, Jennifer," he returned composedly. "Have you forgotten already that we married for mutual convenience? As Mrs. Standish you have my name, my home, my family—" here there was the tiniest lightening of his expression, quickly gone "—and a certain sphere of comfort in a generally uncomfortable world. In turn I have an escape from the endless pleasure hunt of a hollow society to your companionship at home."

He went on in the same coldly dispassionate tone, "That companionship provided the grounds for our marriage, as far as I'm concerned undoubtedly the best grounds for any marriage. I've seen what so-called love can do to a couple, and I'm thankful that we agreed to marry with minds unclouded by destructive emotion."

Jenny choked back a fervent disagreement. Better to have him think she was as coldly detached as he was than to know the truth about her feelings; denied his love, she couldn't tolerate his pity. Still, she was adult enough to know that marriage beds weren't shared only by couples who adored each other, and irresistibly she pleaded for the consolation of at least being allowed to love him wordlessly.

She slipped out of bed and crossed the room to put a hand on his arm. "But Adam, surely we...."

She had forgotten she wore only a wisp of white nylon, and as he looked at her with an expression of remote disinterest, a hot flush spread across her face, down her neck and onto the soft skin that gleamed through her nightdress. Picking up the negligee that he had left spread on the day bed the night before, Adam handed it to Jenny and said with brutal directness, "We can be good friends, Jennifer, but friends don't sleep together."

He moved away from her, walking with his usual grace, and paused at the door to say politely, "And now, if you'll excuse me, I should be off to the office. Have a pleasant day, and do whatever exploring and settling in you like. I'll see you this afternoon."

Then he was gone, and Jenny stood alone in the middle of the room, clutching her negligee to herself in almost unbearable mortification, staring at the hearth where Adam's fire had gone out as they talked. She made no attempt to relight it, but finally she did wash and dress, putting on with slow, heavy movements whatever clothes came first to her hands. Carrying the tray on which her almost untouched breakfast had sadly congealed, she stepped into the hall and, her face averted, passed the door that must have led to Adam's room.

Downstairs she located the kitchen at the back of the house. Timothy and his wife were finishing their morning tea. Mrs. Brown rose and took Jenny's tray, clucking, "Now, Mrs. Standish, there was no need for you to bring that down yourself; I would have come for it in a bit."

Trying to behave normally, Jenny managed something of a smile and said, ''I wanted to thank you for my breakfast.''

Mrs. Brown's shrewd eyes noted that the breakfast was almost completely uneaten, but she didn't comment on it, putting Jenny's lack of appetite down to a surfeit of excitement the day before. She said, ''Mr. Standish prefers to have his breakfast down here, but I'll be happy to bring you up a tray every morning if you'd like.''

''Thank you, that would be perfect, Mrs. Brown,'' Jenny said gratefully. How could she possibly face Adam each morning across the breakfast table? If only there was some plausible excuse for also having dinner in her room each night! Of course there was none, though, and when Mrs. Brown showed her the menu for that night's dinner she just read it through and handed it back with a nod. ''That sounds delicious.''

The little woman beamed, and Jenny added, ''I don't really need to see the menu for each day, Mrs. Brown. You probably know my husband's tastes and preferences far better than I do, and I'm sure anything you serve us will be excellent.''

''All right, Mrs. Standish. Shall I make lunch for you today?''

Deciding quickly that she couldn't bear to spend the whole day in the house, Jenny answered, ''Thank you, no. I think I'll have a look around the house and then go for a walk and perhaps do some shopping.'' And with a little wave she escaped from the cozy kitchen and the Browns' friendly interest.

She did spend a short while exploring Adam's house, which was situated in an area of attractive and fashionable buildings that had once quartered first hawks and then horses. Each of the other rooms downstairs had Oriental carpets and fine eighteenth-century furniture, which attested to Adam's good taste: he certainly didn't need a wife to help him decorate his exquisite home. She spent the least time in the paneled library where Adam had brought her for coffee that evening in the summer, preferring not to think back to the time when she had first begun falling in love with him. Finished with the lower rooms, she crossed the striking black and white parquet floor of the foyer and climbed the stairs, glancing into the guest bedroom at the front of the house before returning to her own room; as well as Adam's there were two other rooms for Timothy and his wife.

In her own pretty bedroom, Jenny looked listlessly around and then began to unpack the cases she had brought from Repose. In her dressing room she filled more drawers and used more hangers, adding the older clothes to those of her trousseau. When she had finished she put on an attractive russet tweed coat, snatched up her handbag and gloves and fled from the house.

She walked for hours, covering miles in an attempt to work off her humiliation and unhappiness. Eventually she was able to drum up some anger and resolution to protect her from her hopeless love for Adam. If he wanted only a tepid companionship from her, then she would give him just that and somehow prevent herself from showing him anything more. She had been cruelly hurt that morning, and she would not—could not—leave herself open for such rejection again.

It was well into the afternoon by the time Jenny managed to put herself into this frame of mind; she ate a late lunch at a small restaurant and took a cab back to the mews. When Adam arrived, she greeted him with cool courtesy and carried on a pleasant, inconsequential conversation during tea. Later, she got through Mrs. Brown's dinner in the same poised way, a charming and slightly unreal companion. She kept Adam company by the library fire for an hour or so after dinner, reading while he worked on some papers, then wished him a polite good evening and went upstairs to her solitary bed, where she flung herself down and cried softly until all her tears were spent.   By the time he came upstairs, her room was dark and still. He had no way of knowing that she lay awake most of the night.

CHAPTER ELEVEN

THAT FIRST DAY of Jenny's married life set a pattern for many other days. Adam would stop in for a brief goodbye while she breakfasted in her room, and then the hours would stretch emptily in front of her. She fell into the habit of carrying down her breakfast tray every morning and staying a little while in the gleaming, modern kitchen to visit with the Browns in whose undemanding company she found relief. Then she might arrange a vase of flowers or write a few letters that revealed to Dr. Pennington, Miss Mayfair and the family at Repose nothing about the monotony of her life. Knowing that Mrs. Brown delighted in cooking for her, she usually stayed at home for lunch, not escaping from the house until she had eaten.

At first she spent her afternoons shopping for things she didn't really need and taking long, aimless walks; then in desperation she resorted to her hobby of those early days in London and explored a few more areas that could be reached by subway. She also found consolation for her loneliness by visiting several of the city's famous museums, beginning with the huge British Museum. There, the presence of such historical treasures as the *Anglo-Saxon Chronicle* and the manuscript of *Beowulf* made her feel close to her father and a little less lonely.

When Adam was at home, she forced herself to be an attentive and entertaining companion, recounting for him some of her daytime expeditions and discoveries with much of the same fluency of words that had characterized Owen Tremayne's best writing. Only when she was sure he was out of earshot did she let herself cry in her room for shattered hopes and stifled love. Adam never knew of her tears; but he did see the honing down of her face, so that her delicate cheekbones protruded under the translucent skin. He said nothing about it, however, but when she wasn't looking he watched her with a brooding tension.

About two weeks after her wedding, Jenny received a note from Blair Graham. He wrote diffidently to remind her about his exhibition and to invite her and Adam to the opening. Over dinner that night she told her husband about the invitation.

"This is that painter you rented your house to?" he asked, his black eyebrows lowered thoughtfully. She nodded. "Is he any good?"

She heard the light skepticism lacing his tone and answered coolly, "I think so, but I've no idea whether or not you would agree."

"When did you say it was?"

She told him again, and he responded with a small shrug. "Well, in that case, we won't find out if I agree or not, because I won't be free to go with you. You should certainly go by yourself, though, if you think you'd be interested.

Sitting there, separated from her husband by far more than the length of polished table between them, drearily conscious of the uniform gray of the London winter outside, Jenny was swept by the memory of those golden autumn days in Cornwall when she had still thought that perhaps her marriage to Adam would become something more than he had proposed. Blair's easy company had been part of those hopeful, sunlit days, and she found she was looking forward to seeing him again, even though she knew nothing would recapture what she had lost since they last met.

Unaware that she was weaving her fingers together in her lap, she answered Adam quietly, "Yes, I think I will go."

When the day of the opening arrived, Jenny dressed with great care. After some indecision she finally put on an elegant, carnation pink wool dress, hoping its soft color would conceal from Blair the pallor of her skin. She also added a touch of pink to her lips and cheekbones, then tucked her hair into a neat coil at the nape of her neck. Slipping her feet into shoes that were both pretty and comfortable, she picked up gloves and purse, then shrugged into her stylish navy coat. After one last critical look she decided she looked far different from the windblown Cornish girl of the previous fall; she only hoped Blair would attribute the change to city clothes and the different season.

Because of the time she had taken dressing, Jenny found that when she arrived at the gallery a considerable number of people were already there. Blair himself was surrounded by friends, many from his art-school days, and she was able to speak with him only for a moment when she came in.

On her own, she spent a long time looking at the paintings attractively displayed around the small but well-known gallery. Blair's talent was even more powerful than she remembered, and he had caught, with quiet certainty, the curiously luminous quality of Cornwall.

Preserved forever in the eternity of paint were glittering, hazy days when the veiled sun glinted silver on Cornish waves, and cool, clear evenings when a slanting sunset poured molten gold across a rocky land. Wind-twisted hawthorne trees fought to keep their precarious hold in thin soil, and donkeys roamed where the stone cromlechs concealed the secrets of the ancient people who built them.

Lost in memories, Jenny moved slowly from canvas to canvas. It was all there—the places Blair had found for himself and those they had seen together. Several of the pictures included a dark-haired girl that Jenny knew unself-consciously was herself, as she was then. . . .

It was nearly two hours later when Jenny reluctantly returned from the timeless magic of Cornwall to the present reality of London. With a little sigh, she began to move toward the door, but before she reached it Blair wove his way across the room toward her. When he reached her, she held out her hand, which he took in both of his, holding it wordlessly. Jenny was the first to speak, in a tone she made light. "Blair, what a wonderful show!"

"It couldn't have happened without you," he answered gravely, looking not at her but at the hand he still held. She pulled it gently but firmly free.

"Nonsense. All I did was let you rent my house when you needed it and show you some places you would eventually have found on your own."

"And give me back the joy in painting I lost while lying in a hospital bed."

Uncertain how to respond to this, she was quiet for a moment while groups of people eddied around them. She commented finally on the crowd just as someone in it called his name.

He answered with a wave and grinned at Jenny. "Yes, all my old friends from art school turned out to make sure I had a suitable mob for my opening! The only drawback to so many loyal supporters is that they don't leave me with much time to talk to anyone. Jenny, could you have lunch with me tomorrow? Would your husband miss you?"

Miss her? The words sank tiger claws into Jenny, and she had a sudden urge to blurt into Blair's kindly face the truth that Adam wouldn't miss her at lunch, or dinner, or any other time. Instead, she said only, "Oh, no, Adam doesn't come home for lunch, so I generally have it by myself."

Pride had prevented her bitter little outburst, and she made her tone casual. Blair heard the tone, but his perceptive eye also saw the momentary tightening of her face that preceded it. Both too wise and too polite to question her about it, he merely said, "Good. Could you meet me here, and we'll make up our minds where to eat then?"

She agreed, and he saw her outside to a cab, waving her off with a smile that changed into a thoughtful frown when she was no longer close enough to see his expression.

Somewhat to Jenny's surprise Adam remembered that evening at dinner to ask what she had thought of the exhibition. Across her mind flashed a series of brilliant and evocative paintings, but she said coolly, "Oh, it was rather good," reluctant for some reason to voice the praise it deserved lest Adam decide to see for himself. She hesitated an instant and then added casually, "Blair asked me to lunch with him tomorrow, and I agreed if you have no objections?"

He paused to sip his wine before replying in the echo of her own unconcerned tone, "Objection? Of course not. In a marriage like ours that would be an inexcusably Victorian attitude. Enjoy your luncheon."

In fact, Jenny did enjoy it. Of course Blair couldn't know how much in need of cheering she was these days, but in the small restaurant they had decided on he was as amusing and delightful as if he had deliberately set out to raise her spirits. He entertained her with outrageous stories of his escapades in art school, and Jenny laughed until she was breathless. Briefly, she was able to forget the heartbreaking situation of her marriage, and Blair saw again the enchanting girl he had known in Cornwall.

After lunch they shared a cab as far as the gallery, where Blair disembarked. Before he left her, he said, "Jenny, I've enjoyed this so much. Is there any chance you could join me for lunch again on Friday?"

Hearing in her mind Adam's voice saying calmly, "In a marriage like ours . . ." and seeing before her Blair's friendly face, Jenny felt a moment of rebellion. While it lasted she replied quickly, "Of course. I'd like to come."

That evening Adam either didn't remember or didn't choose to ask Jenny about her lunch with Blair, treating her with grave courtesy but asking no questions. Uncertain at first whether to be relieved or disappointed at that, she volunteered no information and didn't notice a tautness in Adam's face whenever he looked at her. By Friday she had decided that he asked no questions because he simply wasn't interested, and so she went off to her appointment with Blair in a mood of defiant misery.

The city was experiencing a few days of unseasonably warm weather, and when Jenny arrived at the art gallery Blair produced a picnic basket and said with a slightly apologetic laugh, "In weather like this I couldn't resist the temptation."

They had their picnic in St. James's Park, and Jenny tried gallantly to match her companion's spirits. She wasn't very successful, and gradually he, too, became quieter. Finally, he spoke into a silence that was becoming awkward.

"Jenny." She looked up from the clasped hands she had been studying, and because she couldn't banish Adam from her mind that day her face was desolate. "Jenny, don't look like that!"

The note of urgency in Blair's voice broke through her unhappiness enough to make her look closely at him. The rumpled red hair was grayer than she remembered, and the expression in his brown eyes was one she didn't recognize. Then he spoke more calmly.

"I hate to see you unhappy, and I can't help but see that you are. Is there anything I can do to help? Anything at all, Jenny."

The words, though kind, were unremarkable, but as she watched his face Jenny realized with a sudden sense of shock that he loved her.

She bent her head so that he couldn't see her eyes filling with tears. Mixed with a sort of humble amazement at his feelings for her were both pity, because she had to hurt him, and despair, because she loved Adam instead of Blair. If only she could have changed the course of events! If only she had fallen in love with Blair, with his warm and giving nature, instead of Adam, with his distant and difficult one!

When she finally spoke, her voice was indistinct, and Blair had to lean toward her bent head to hear it. "Thank you, Blair, from the bottom of my heart, but no, there's nothing you can do."

A question had been asked and an answer given, and Blair sat back; there was nothing more he could say. A few moments later Jenny shivered and he said evenly, "It's getting colder. Shall we go?"

Jenny nodded and gathered the remains of their picnic, and as she stood up Blair buttoned her coat around her as if she were a beloved child. She finally looked up at him, standing passively while he worked his way down the buttons, and in her eyes he could see both her love for Adam and her regret.

When he had finished, they both stood motionless for a moment, then he said quietly, "I think it's time I went back to Cornwall," and kissed her briefly on the lips. In a few minutes she was in a cab for home, and Blair had gone out of her life. Back in her room in the mews she wept for a fate that decreed that she, hurt by a hopeless love, should inflict the same punishment on another.

By the time Adam came home, she was in control of herself again, and during the next few days she returned to her program of solitary exploration of the city. Occasionally she thought with a sad humor that soon she'd know London as well as a professional tour guide.

Because she spent comparatively little time with him, it

took Jenny a day or so to become aware that Adam had caught a severe cold. It was early February, and at first he seemed only irritable, so she put it down to the weather, now seasonably cold again, its depressing wetness limiting her explorations. But when he arrived home with a flushed face and a racking cough, there was no longer any doubt that he was quite ill. He ate little and said less but was often shaken with tearing paroxysms of coughing. He made no effort to see a doctor and refused even to stay home from the office the next day.

Inescapably, Jenny remembered the untreated influenza that had taken her father, and she became thoroughly frightened about Adam's condition. That evening after the Browns had gone to their own quarters she fixed him a hot cup of soup, but he refused to touch it; when she suggested he go to bed early he snapped, "I'm not your child, Jennifer, so don't try to mother me."

Worried but helpless, she sank into her chair by the library fire and made a pretense of reading the magazine she had picked up, all the while conscious of Adam's noisy breathing. Finally she put down the magazine and bade him a quiet good night.

In her room a few minutes later she was relieved to hear him coming slowly up the stairs. She heard him moving around in the next room for a little while, and then he must have gone to bed because there was no sound for a time. She herself curled up on the ivory day bed and, too worried to sleep, stared into the flames leaping in the fireplace. Soon she heard him begin to toss and turn, coughing incessantly all the while.

It was hours before the next room was quiet again, and Jenny crawled exhaustedly into bed. She was still heavy-eyed in the morning when Adam came to her door to say goodbye. Wearily pushing back her hair, she said hesitantly,

"Adam, must you go to the office today? If someone has to be there, couldn't your father come? I know he would if he knew you were ill."

"I don't like to ask him on such short notice, especially when I'm not so sick I need to stay home. For God's sake, don't fuss over me, Jennifer," he rapped out. Then he said a curt goodbye and went downstairs, and she heard him cough again before he left the house.

Jenny spent an aimless day. The weather was still too inclement for walking, and Adam's lovely house began to seem like a cage. After her morning visit with the Browns, she prowled restlessly, unable to settle down.

She was relieved to see Adam looking better when he finally came home. But he seemed to be just as irascible as ever, and Jenny quickly decided to leave him alone. She said good night right after dinner and left him sitting peevishly in the library. In her own room she changed into a pretty nightgown from her trousseau, then sat by the fire, an unopened book in her hands.

She dozed a little, and when she awoke the fire had died and she could hear Adam pacing the room below. She shivered a little in her thin gown and glanced at the clock on her desk. It was well past midnight; why was Adam still up at this hour? Without a proper amount of sleep, he was more likely to have a relapse than a recovery.

Still only half-awake herself, Jenny slid to her feet and went to her door, forgetting robe and slippers. She padded quietly down the steps and opened the library door, saying before she lost her courage, "Adam, please, with that terrible cold you should be in bed."

From the far side of the room he looked at her, and then Jenny noticed the brandy snifter in his hand; the bottle stood open on a tray nearby. He saw the direction of her glance and held up his glass, one eyebrow raised sardonically. "Best treatment for a cold I can think of," he said, and she was startled to hear a faint slurring to his words. They usually had wine with dinner, but other than that she had never seen Adam drink more than a glass of sherry before the meal or a liqueur afterward.

But she stood her ground and repeated, "Adam, I'm not trying to mother you, but you really should be in bed."

"So should you," he retorted, letting his eyes roam lazily up and down the thin nightgown that suggested as much as it covered. "We should both be in bed."

Scarlet with embarrassment, Jenny was annoyed with herself for coming downstairs without a robe. She remembered only too clearly Adam's cruelty the last time he had seen her like that. Nevertheless, she was still worried about him and reluctant to give up.

While she hesitated, he put his glass carefully on the mantelpiece and walked over to the tray. A second glass stood beside the bottle, which he filled and handed to Jenny with exaggerated courtesy. "To keep you warm even without a robe," he said, then returned to his own glass.

Still trying to think of a way to make Adam see sense, Jenny sipped uncertainly at her brandy and felt it burn its way down her throat. Almost immediately its warmth spread through her; she hadn't realized how chilled she was.

As she sipped thoughtfully, Adam watched her, a shuttered look to his face, and then he moved to stand in front of her. "Shall we drink a toast?" he asked in that mocking voice, and Jenny nodded cautiously.

"A toast, then, Jenny," he said, and suddenly a reckless note came into his voice. "A toast to friendship and married friends who sleep alone!"

While Jenny stood motionless, looking over the rim of her glass with startled blue eyes, he drained his own and, with a sudden gesture, flung it into the fireplace. It shattered, and then, except for the crackling of the fire and the sound of their uneven breathing, the room was silent.

At last, in a thickened voice Adam said, "Oh God, why did I ever think we could be just friends?" and with a smothered groan he took her in his arms, burying his face in the tumbled warmth of her hair and then, with a sort of desperation, finding her lips. Her glass fell unnoticed to the rug and lay there spreading a small puddle while Jenny, crushed against Adam's chest, returned his kisses with equal intensity. Nothing else mattered except the closeness and rising passion of their two bodies; all the estrangement and unhappiness were washed away by a wave of feeling that broke free at last.

A short time later Adam freed his lips for a moment, in spite of Jenny's murmured protest, and clouded gray eyes looked at her as she lay cradled in his arms. With a tiny smile she put up one hand and traced a winged eyebrow; he caught the hand and kissed it, his breath warm on her palm, then breathed against her skin, "Guinevere?"

"Yes," she whispered and heard his breath catch. Then she relaxed against him, and he slipped his arms under her shoulders and knees, lifting her tightly against him with hands that were warm through the filmy nylon of her nightgown and carried her upstairs to his room.

JENNY AWOKE SOFTLY, her head pillowed on Adam's shoulder and his arm curled loosely around her. Her mind drugged with happiness, she stayed as she was for a few minutes, looking sleepily around Adam's dim room for the first time. It had a spacious emptiness to it, being rather Spartanly furnished; a very masculine room, its only note of luxury was the wide bed on which they lay.

Her hand resting on Adam's chest rose and fell with his slow breathing, and she watched it with drowsy pleasure, but then gradually realized that the skin she touched was still slightly too warm. A slow smile crept across her face as she recalled the results of her concern for his health last night. She eased herself up onto one elbow and couldn't resist feathering a kiss across the smooth skin over his collarbone. He murmured as she did so and she gently stroked with tender fingers the unruly black hair away from his forehead. He did not awake, and with the probing gray eyes closed, his face had a curious innocence; she felt a surge of love for both the man he was and the child he must have been. Finally, after a last delighted look, she curled up tightly by his side and was soon asleep, a little smile on her lips.

When she awoke again, it was late morning and she was alone in the bed. Mrs. Brown was hovering uncertainly in the doorway with a breakfast tray in her hands. Jenny struggled up against the pillows and said, "Oh, good morning, Mrs. Brown. Have I overslept?"

Seeing she was awake at last, the little woman bustled in and settled the tray across Jenny's knees, saying, "Yes, ma'am, but Mr. Standish told us not to wake you."

"Oh, has he left for work already?" Jenny asked, not knowing how disappointed her voice sounded.

Mrs. Brown smiled warmly, glad to see the two young people behaving more like the newlyweds they were: Mr. Standish had looked uncommonly cheerful that morning, and here was the young lady missing him the minute she woke up. She said comfortingly, "He asked me to be sure to tell you he'd be home early this evening. Oh, and a box arrived for you just a few minutes ago. Shall I bring it up?"

"Yes, please," Jenny answered, wondering what it could be.

Mrs. Brown left the room and reappeared a minute later—puffing slightly from her quick trip up the stairs—with

a long white box in her arms. She placed it on the bed, and
Jenny untied the gold cord with eager fingers. Lifting the lid,
she parted the tissue paper and revealed a shining profusion
of white roses.

She drew in her breath and reached for the card as
Mrs. Brown said admiringly, "My, aren't they lovely?"
then added teasingly, "From one of your admirers, I suppose?"

Jenny lifted glowing eyes from the card—which said
simply "Like a white wave of joy, Guinevere. Love, Adam"
in his angular handwriting—and answered, "Yes, my husband!"

"Now, isn't that nice. Well, I'll take these roses
downstairs and find a vase for them." And with a last,
sympathetic smile at Jenny's pleasure, Mrs. Brown returned
to the kitchen.

Jenny lingered over her breakfast tray for once, savoring
each mouthful and thinking delightedly about the roses her
husband had sent. Over and over, she read the few words on
Adam's card, rejoicing in them.

Finally she finished the last of her tea and scrambled out of
bed. A quick bath, then she slipped on an emerald green shirtwaist dress that highlighted the glow of her skin. A touch of
lipstick on a face whose radiance needed nothing else, a clip
in hastily brushed hair, and she was ready to go downstairs.

In the neat kitchen she found that Mrs. Brown had
unearthed a large green cut-glass vase into which she had
placed the roses. The two women chatted companionably
while Jenny fussed happily with her flowers. When they were
finally arranged to her satisfaction, she picked up the vase
carefully and began to prowl the downstairs rooms, trying it
first in one place and then another. She wound up in the
library and with an absurd feeling of whimsy put the roses on
the low table on which Adam's brandy bottle had stood the

night before. She laughed at herself but, stepping back, realized the flowers looked lovely there, glowing against the paneling behind.

Outside, the weather was still cold and wet, the temperature nearly down to freezing, but for once Jenny was entirely content to stay in the little house. She drifted smilingly from room to room and after a late lunch finally settled in the library, where the delightful scent of the roses wafted all around her as she stared dreamily into the fire and waited for her husband.

She didn't stir when the telephone rang, knowing that Timothy or his wife would answer it, and she still hadn't moved when they both entered the room. Looking up, she saw that Timothy's forehead was deeply creased and his wife's lips were quivering. The look of reverie fled from Jenny's face, and she rose swiftly to her feet. "What is it? Has something happened to Adam?"

Timothy walked forward and put a steadying hand on her shoulder, answering first the question she hadn't dared ask. "He's alive, Mrs. Standish, but there was an accident. The police just called. The roads were icy, and as he was coming home, a truck skidded up on the curb and fell over onto his car."

Jenny's breath whistled through her clenched teeth, and she saw in her mind's eye the beautiful green Jaguar, crushed and bent around Adam's body. Suddenly the room began to darken around her and she thought she was going to faint.

When she could see clearly again, she was back in her chair, her head lowered and Mrs. Brown holding her tightly so she wouldn't fall. She stirred against Mrs. Brown's motherly bosom, then managed in a tight little voice, "Where is he? Can I see him?"

"The ambulance was just taking him to the hospital when

the police called, and they said you could come down there to wait if you liked.''

"Wait?''

Timothy cleared his throat. "He was unconscious, Mrs. Standish, and they couldn't say how long it might be before he came to.''

Jenny turned her head away again for a minute and when the kindly Mrs. Brown murmured soothingly, "There, love, it'll be all right,'' she burst into a storm of weeping.

Mrs. Brown let her cry it out, and finally Jenny was in control again. A worried Timothy handed her his large white handkerchief, and she mopped her tear-stained face, saying brokenly, "I'm sorry—''

"Never mind, dear,'' interrupted Mrs. Brown. "It's probably done you some good, and it certainly hasn't done us any harm.''

Jenny managed a small watery smile at her bracing tone, then looked at Timothy and asked, "Would you call me a cab, please?''

"No, ma'am, that I won't,'' he said firmly. "We have our own little car that Mr. Standish lets up keep here, and we'll drive you ourselves.''

Jenny looked at him gratefully, and his wife helped her to her feet and went for her coat and handbag.

CHAPTER TWELVE

ALL THAT NIGHT Jenny sat in Adam's darkened hospital room, watching by his bed. The night sister checked on him at regular intervals, and twice the house surgeon came by. But Adam didn't regain consciousness, and he was unaware of Jenny holding one of his hands very tightly.

She was still holding it the next morning when the doctors gathered at Adam's bed. His broken ribs had been taped, and his concussion didn't seem serious, but there was some question as to whether or not his spine had been injured. The doctors talked quietly for a few minutes at the foot of Adam's bed, then the resident medical officer stepped over to Jenny's side and urged her to go home for a few hours' rest.

"Your husband may not wake for a while yet, and we'd rather not have you on our hands as a patient, too," he explained with kindly concern. Reluctantly Jenny agreed.

She had promised the Browns she would let Timothy come for her when she was ready to go home, so she slipped out and phoned him, then returned to Adam's room to wait. It seemed only a few minutes later that both the Browns arrived and led her gently away.

At home Jenny collapsed in her own bed and slept heavily for four hours, waking unrefreshed but too worried to stay in bed. She dressed absentmindedly and went downstairs where she ate a meal without enjoyment. Afterward she went to the telephone and called first the hospital, which reported that Adam was still unconscious, and then David and Anne at Repose.

She was too distraught to be anything but blunt, and when Anne answered she said baldly, ''Anne, it's Jenny. Adam's been hurt in a car crash; he's unconscious. Can you and David come here?''

She heard Anne's quick gasp, quickly followed by, ''Certainly, love. I'll get someone to stay here with Teddy and we'll leave immediately. Should we come to the house or straight to the hospital?''

Knowing she wouldn't be able to stay away from Adam's bedside, Jenny told Anne to go to the hospital, and giving her instructions for getting there, she hung up.

Thanks to the unobtrusive help of the Browns, Jenny was back at the hospital when Anne and David arrived in midafternoon. They entered the room quietly, and Jenny stood to meet them. D vid took her hand for a minute in a fierce clasp, and Anne hugged her warmly. At last Jenny freed herself, saying in a voice that wobbled a little, ''You'll start me crying again if you're not careful.''

Then she explained in a low tone what had happened and the apparent extent of Adam's injuries. ''A concussion and broken ribs don't frighten me that much,'' she said forlornly. ''It's the possibility of damage to his spine . . . and he's been unconscious for so long.''

They spoke in whispers a while longer, trying to encourage each other, then Jenny suggested to David that he might stop by the offices of the publishing company. His face was so strained and white as he looked at his unconscious son that she had begun to worry about him, as well, and made her suggestion in hope that his tension would be eased a bit if he had something to do. Only when she admitted she had forgotten to call the office and tell them what had happened to Adam did David agree to go, and he left with a last anxious look at the still figure on the bed.

When he had gone, Anne looked at Jenny and nodded a

wordless agreement with her strategy for David, then she pulled another chair up by Jenny's and sat quietly with her. They hardly spoke at all, but Jenny found the other woman's sympathetic presence a comfort.

Finding when he returned two hours later that Adam had still not regained consciousness, David suggested that Anne and Jenny come down to the hospital cafeteria with him for a sandwich. Jenny had no appetite at all, but Anne—and common sense—argued that she'd be of no use to Adam if she fainted from hunger, so with a word to the staff nurse she consented to go.

The three of them ate mechanically and discussed what they should do. Over her coffee cup, Anne looked at Jenny. "What do you mean to do now? Why not go home and get some sleep? You look as though you haven't had any in a week, love."

"Anne, I can't. I couldn't sleep anyway, and I'd rather stay with Adam so I can be there—when he wakes up."

Anne set down her coffee cup and stretched a warm hand across to Jenny, reading the fearful thought in her mind. "All right; we understand. Perhaps we should go to a hotel and grab some sleep ourselves; then we could relieve you in the morning if necessary."

"Yes, but don't stay in a hotel; please use our guest bedroom in the mews."

Anne exchanged a thoughtful look with David, and he said, "If you're sure we'll be no trouble. . . ."

"No, of course you won't be any trouble. I'll call the Browns and tell them you're coming. They're dear people, and I think they'll be just as glad to have something to do."

When she called, the Browns confirmed Jenny's guess, and it was settled. David and Anne walked Jenny back to Adam's room and left her there to keep her silent vigil.

Once, late that second night, Adam stirred slightly, and

she leaned over him to call his name softly, but he didn't respond at all. With a sigh, she sank back in her chair and tried not to be afraid.

In the morning the same kindly doctor sent her home again, but this time she took a cab rather than phoning Timothy. She reached home just as David and Anne were finishing breakfast, and after Jenny had a cup of tea and a few bites of toast Anne took her upstairs and tucked her in as though she were a little girl. Standing by Jenny's bed, she said softly, "David and I will go keep watch, love. Sleep as long as you can." Then she switched off the light and slipped out of the room.

Knowing they were with Adam and being completely exhausted, Jenny did sleep, a heavy, drugged sleep. It was late afternoon when she awoke, and after she'd had a light meal Timothy dropped her off at the hospital.

She found David and Anne leaning wearily against the wall in the corridor outside Adam's room. Hearing the sound of her footsteps, they looked up. She was too frightened to speak, but David put a tired arm across her shoulders and answered the panic-stricken question in her eyes. "No. He's conscious, Jenny, and he knew who we were. There's a consultant with him now."

Jenny sagged a little against him, and he held her tightly while Anne gave her a faint understanding smile. The consultant was in Adam's room for a long time, and when he finally came out he spoke first to Anne and David. "He'd like to see you."

David introduced Jenny briefly to the tall man with keen blue eyes and close-cropped, iron gray hair. "Jenny, this is Dr. Llewellyn, who's taking Adam's case; Dr. Llewellyn, Adam's wife, Jennifer Standish." Then he and Anne quietly entered Adam's room, and the door shut behind them while the consultant walked with Jenny slowly along the corridor.

"As you know, Mrs. Standish, your husband regained consciousness this afternoon. He's rather weak but perfectly coherent, confirming that his concussion was no more severe than we thought. His ribs should mend nicely, so you have no cause to worry on that account, but...."

He stopped walking, and Jenny paused beside him. "Mrs. Standish, how long have you been married?"

"Five weeks," she answered, puzzled by this sudden turning of the conversation.

"The wedding flowers hardly faded," he murmured, looking at her considerately. Then he took her arm and began walking again. "I'm sorry to give you some rather difficult news just now, but as we feared, there has been some damage to your husband's spine. I think that once his other injuries heal and his condition has stabilized, I'll be able to operate on him with a good chance of success, but for the time being his legs are paralyzed."

Jenny's face whitened at the last word, and she stumbled a little, but the firm clasp on her arm didn't loosen, and Dr. Llewellyn kept her walking slowly along the corridor. He said nothing more for a few minutes, giving her time to deal with the shock.

Finally she said, "What can I do for him?" and the hand at her elbow squeezed briefly.

"Good girl. I was looking for that reaction. You can do a great deal. I'm going to ask you to see that he doesn't lose heart. I may have to do more than one operation to give your husband back full use of his legs, and the operations are very delicate. I won't hide from you the fact that there is some element of risk in them; however, I am personally confident of eventual success if he is otherwise healthy in both body and mind. His bones must knit, and his desire for success must be strong. I have no worries about him physically, but his mental state concerns me.

"Frankly, Mrs. Standish, he isn't taking this well. He seems possessed by the notion that my talk of operations is only talk, meant to hide from him the truth that he'll never walk again."

Jenny's heart contracted in love and pity, and Dr. Llewellyn faced her. "He *is* wrong, however, and I'll need you to convince him of that."

Through Jenny's mind flashed the memory of Adam carrying her up the stairs only three nights before, and she had an instant's perfect comprehension of what it would mean to him to be crippled. Her gentle mouth tightened into a firm line, and she nodded to the man beside her. "I'll do everything I can."

The consultant said only, "Good," and together they walked back along the corridor toward Adam's room. As they neared the door, it opened and David and Anne emerged.

Jenny sped up her steps and words bubbled from her. "How is he? Is he asking for me?"

David's shoulders sagged, and Anne looked at her with eyes full of love and pain; then she turned and addressed Dr. Llewellyn in a low voice, leading him off down the corridor again while Jenny spoke in a tone sharp with fear. "David, what is it? What's wrong? Is Adam worse?" The staccato questions shot out.

He shook his head in answer to the last question but slipped an arm around her waist and led her to a small waiting room nearby before he spoke. Over by a high window that looked out onto a gray courtyard, he turned her to face him, taking both her cold hands in his warm ones.

"Physically he is no worse, Jenny; he was able to talk to us without too much discomfort, and his condition was stable as I'm sure the doctor told you. The worst problem isn't physical; it's mental."

"Yes, I know," Jenny said in impatient bewilderment. "Dr. Llewellyn said he was despressed and would need me to keep his spirits up."

David sighed and tightened his hold on her hands. "I'm sure it's true Jenny, but not just yet, that's all."

She started to speak. "Not yet...?"

"He won't see you, my dear; he asked us to take you home immediately."

Stunned into silence, Jenny searched his face. Around his compassionate eyes, bluer than his son's, were deep lines; other lines were etched at the corners of his mouth, and he looked suddenly older.

"I'm sorry, Jenny," he said softly, and she nodded, struggling with the desolation inside her.

Turning her head, she stared blindly out the windows for a long time, seeing nothing of the barren courtyard. As no alternative occurred to her and she wanted only what her husband wanted, she said finally in a lifeless voice, "Shall we go then?"

"I'll get Anne. Wait here a moment, dear," and with a last reassuring squeeze he released her hands. He returned with his wife almost immediately, and they led Jenny, moving like a sleepwalker, out to David's car.

Back in Ennismore Mews, David explained the situation briefly to the Browns while Anne took Jenny upstairs. Treating her as though she were Joan's age or younger, she ran a hot bath for the white-faced girl, then closed the ivory drapes and built a cheerful fire to combat the bleakness outdoors and in Jenny's heart. When Jenny emerged from the bathroom, her hair curling damply at the tips, a tiny bit of color in her cheeks from the bath, Anne tucked her into bed and poured her a cup of the steaming tea brought by a worried Mrs. Brown.

"I'm glad to see you're looking a little less spent, love,"

she said while Jenny sipped, "and now I want you to listen to me. Adam's actions this afternoon were a shock to all of us, and especially to you, but I think we're all unduly upset."

At Jenny's indignant gasp, she grinned briefly. "No, let me explain before you let fly at me! We're all losing sight of the fact that after being unconscious for two days Adam woke up this afternoon to find things radically changed from the way they had been. Instead of being at home with the wife he loves—Mrs. Brown pointed out your roses, by the way—he wakes up in a hospital bed and discovers he can't use his legs. Along comes some fellow who says he's sure operations can fix everything up, but he can't offer an absolute guarantee and he can't operate at all until some unspecified time in the future. Hit with all that at once, after two days of wandering in who knows what far-off subconscious countries, he's distraught, and is it any wonder? We have to remember what he's just been through and give him time to become adjusted and be himself again.

"And now, Jenny my love, I want you to take one of these tablets Dr. Llewellyn gave me to help you sleep. No arguments, either; when Adam's ready to see you, he won't want to see a washed-out ghost!"

Somewhat cheered by Anne's line of reasoning, Jenny smiled and meekly accepted the pill, then slipped under the covers. Anne stayed beside her, chattering nonsense, until the sleeping pill began to take effect. Then she kissed Jenny's cheek and moved to the door, saying softly as she switched off the light, "Be patient, my dear. A day or two, and he'll want to see you."

CHAPTER THIRTEEN

BUT HE DIDN'T.

The days fell into a pattern. Each morning David went in to the publishing offices while Anne kept Jenny company. The three would lunch together in the mews, then David and Anne would go to the hospital while Jenny fretted at home. When they returned at teatime, she'd be waiting for them at the door to ask eagerly, "Will he see me? May I go to him?" Whichever one of them gave it, the answer was always no, and she would droop and turn away.

After two weeks of this, David answered Jenny's question as usual and added as she turned away, "Jenny, he's being moved to a nursing home. Dr. Llewellyn thinks he's mending as well as can be expected and doesn't need hospital care now. He should be ready for the first operation in a couple of months, the doctor thinks, although he's still not happy about Adam's state of mind."

As always, Jenny was pathetically grateful for any news of her husband, but she was beginning to wonder desperately *when* he'd see her. Seeing the little quiver to her lips, Anne spoke up. "Jenny, David and I talked it over last night, and we'd like to take you back to Repose with us. David can come to London every day or two to keep things going and check on Adam—the drive isn't too long for him to commute like this for a while. As for me, Adam isn't so fond of me that he can't spare my company, and I should be getting back to Teddy. Our Mrs. Dean says he's fine, but nightly telephone calls aren't as satisfactory as being able to keep track of him in person. The twins have simply been staying at school, on the weekends, too, and I'd rather like to have them home so I can be sure all's well in that department, too.

"I won't leave you here alone, though, to mope and grieve with only the Browns for company; they can take care of things here while we take care of you at home."

Jenny hesitated, knowing how she'd feel here in London after they left, but hoping against hope that if she stayed Adam might change his mind.

Anne seemed to read her thoughts. "If Adam wants to see you, dear, David can let you know just as easily if you're at Repose." She paused, then went on, "I meant what I said about not leaving unless you come with us, so take pity on poor Mrs. Dean, who's probably been run ragged by our Teddy by now and would love to have us home. You see, I'm not above using a bit of blackmail!"

Jenny smiled a little at Anne's raillery and finally gave in.

At Repose the next evening, while their parents talked to the long-suffering Mrs. Dean about Teddy's misadventures, the children flung themselves on Jenny with glad cries. Then they remembered why she had come and suddenly sobered. Making himself spokesman, Geoffrey said solemnly, "We're awfully sorry Adam's hurt, Jenny," and Joan nodded while Teddy looked at her with big eyes.

She hugged them all to hide the tears that sprang to her eyes, then let them lead her upstairs to the room that had been hers since the first time she'd visited. It was also the room where she had dressed for her wedding, but she tried not to think about that.

Jenny slipped easily into the family circle at Repose. While the twins were at school during the week, she spent time with Teddy and helped Anne with the cooking—as much as the latter would allow. As spring arrived, she helped outdoors a great deal, too, taking charge of planting the kitchen garden; she found that the gentle sun and steady exercise helped to anesthetize the pain of Adam's continued refusal to see her. David went to London nearly every weekday, and he usually stopped to see his son on the way home, but the news was always the same: Adam was mending slowly, but was still paralyzed and still adamantly opposed to having Jenny visit.

It was the end of March when Jenny fainted. She had been working in the garden, and when she straightened up, her vision suddenly went dark and she crumpled and fell among the tiny plants she'd been weeding. Anne found her there a few minutes later when she came out to announce lunch. She was able to bring Jenny around quickly but insisted on sending her to bed and calling the doctor.

He wasn't with Jenny very long, and as soon as he left, Anne came into the bedroom to find out what he'd said. "Well, what does he think of your fainting in my garden?" she inquired, and Jenny looked up from her hands with eyes that sparkled a brilliant blue.

"Like me, he thinks it was probably because I'm going to have a baby."

"Jenny!" Anne swooped down to hug her. "How wonderful! Is it certain?"

"Nearly. The doctor said he'd confirm it with test results as soon as possible. I'm sure it's true, though; I'd begun to think so quite some time ago."

Anne sat on the edge of the bed, and they talked happily for a while, until Anne said with a laugh, "I think I feel as delighted as you look, Jenny, and David and the children will be thrilled, too."

Then she continued more thoughtfully, "Jenny, if you want to write Adam a letter about this, David could take it in to him. Your news might be just the thing to break through those foolish barriers he's set up."

Jenny pleated the bedspread with her fingers. "I don't

think I'll write just yet,'' she said slowly. ''Somehow I don't feel quite ready to tell Adam. I'd rather wait—at least until the test confirms it.''

''Of course; whatever you want,'' Anne agreed.

As Anne had predicted, the rest of the family was delighted. The twins in particular took it upon themselves to act as Jenny's watchdogs, trailing her around whenever they were home to be sure that she didn't overtire herself. She had all she could do to persuade them that working in the garden was just the sort of mild exercise she needed.

The doctor soon confirmed that Jenny was indeed pregnant, but she still delayed writing Adam, uncertain how to tell him and how he would respond. While she hesitated, though, she also found herself missing him more and more and wanting to share with him the excitement she felt.

Out of habit she continued to ask David whenever he returned from the city if Adam wanted to see her, and one Friday he followed his usual regretful shake of the head with the news that Adam had sent home a letter to her.

Jenny's heart leaped. Surely the waiting was over, and he had remembered at last she was truly his wife and had married him ''in sickness and in health.'' He would be willing to see her, and she could share her joy about the baby. And if only she could talk with him, she was sure she could help him prepare mentally for the operations and convince him that she would love him whether they succeeded or failed.

She opened the letter with fingers that shook with happiness, and the rest of the family crowded eagerly around her, clamoring to share the good news. They fell silent, however, when she finished reading the letter and said nothing, standing motionless as if turned to stone.

Suddenly frightened for her, Anne spoke her name; when she received no response, she took the letter gently from

Jenny's unresisting fingers. The children fell back, puzzled at the sudden change of mood around them, and Anne and David rapidly read Adam's letter.

It was terse and brutally to the point: he wanted Jenny to divorce him and would see to it that she had grounds as soon as possible. In the meantime, he preferred not to see her or have any direct contact by mail. He would see to it that the Browns' salaries and all expenses for the house in the mews were paid; she was welcome to stay there, but he would understand if she chose, instead, to return to Cornwall. Wherever she lived, she would receive a regular monthly allowance. She had only to keep his lawyer informed of her wherabouts. The allowance would cease if and when she married again.

"Did he say anything to you about this?" Anne asked her husband in a low voice.

"Not a word, or I'd have tried to talk him out of it. We talked business, then he asked if I'd mind bringing home a letter to Jenny, and of course I assumed it said she was to come and see him. He never so much as hinted he'd been thinking of this."

He turned to the children and quietly took them to play upstairs in the long gallery while Anne led Jenny to a seat by the fire, still needed in the great hall at this time of year. Jenny sat bonelessly, and Anne chafed her cold hands for a few minutes, searching for words. Finally she sighed and said, "Oh, Jenny, I'm sorry. I can't think what to say or what to do."

There was silence, then Jenny said in a flat, brittle voice, "Apparently the thing Adam means me to do is to forget that we were ever married. He still can't trust me, and so he wants me out of his life. It seems you were right about him in the end, Anne, and I was wrong to think that he might ever change—that he had changed!"

The brittle voice broke at the memory of that one enchanted night when she had been Adam's wife in more than just name, and desperately she asked, "Oh, Anne, where can I hide? Where can I run that the memories won't follow me?"

"You can't just crawl into a corner somewhere, love; you have the baby to think of. Can't you stay here with us? You know we all love you—for yourself, not just because Adam married you."

"I can't, Anne. Please understand. I love all of you, too, but here I'd be constantly reminded of Adam by this house he grew up in. And every time David goes to London and visits him without me, it'll hurt all over again.

"I can't go on living in the mews, either, living in his house, cared for by his servants, and accepting his money as if I were still his wife but pretending he doesn't exist! I would see him at every door. I can't even escape by going home to Cornwall—" The thought of Blair flashed through her mind. "Anne, where can I go?"

Jenny dropped her head in her hands, and Anne said tentatively, "Adam still doesn't know about the baby, does he? Jenny, if he did it might make a difference—"

"No!" Jenny's head came up as she interrupted fiercely. "He mustn't be told! I'll love Adam for the rest of my life, but he made his decision, and I won't have him changing his mind just because he suddenly feels responsible for our child.

"Am I being inconsistent, Anne? I feel as though I want Adam's baby more than ever, but I don't want anything else from him. I've finally realized that I can't settle for anything less than his love, and since I can't have that, I want nothing else he might offer because he feels guilty about leaving me with a child. I can support the baby myself: I have my father's royalties and Blair's rent money, besides my own skills as a secretary."

On the last word Anne's eyes narrowed slightly in

concentration; then she stood up and left the room for a few minutes. When she returned, she had a sheet of paper in her hand and a satisfied expression on her face.

"Jenny, I have an idea. When you spoke just now, you reminded me that only a day or two ago I had a letter from my Aunt Eleanor—you know, the one who lives in Scotland? The one who always sends the children sweaters for Christmas?" At Jenny's nod she went on, "Anyway, she wrote complaining that she's just lost another secretary-companion."

Jenny's face showed a flicker of interest, and Anne continued. "Actually, she's my great-aunt, and a formidable old lady, too. She's eighty if she's a day, and she still runs several charitable organizations and keeps up an enormous correspondence. She hasn't been able to keep a secretary, though, because she demands that they also act as companions, and by the time she's barked at them once or twice they're so frightened of her they don't stay long enough to discover her bark really is worse than her bite. The truth is that she's rather a dear but not inclined to let on, even if it costs her employees, because it amuses her to pose as an eccentric old tartar.

"I mentioned her, Jenny, because I think you might suit her very well. David says you're a superb secretary, and I know you're too level-headed to be intimidated by an old lady with a peculiar sense of humor."

"But the baby, Anne? How would she feel about that?"

"I doubt she'd care one way or the other, and she certainly has enough room for you both. All she really wants is someone who will answer her back; if you do that, she'll be delighted to have you even if you decide to make this baby triplets."

Jenny managed a scrap of a smile for the effort at lightness. Then Anne went on, "She lives in Edinburgh, by the way,

Jenny. You could make a start in a new place, but we'd know where you were and could keep track of you. We don't want to lose you completely, you know."

"I wouldn't let you," Jenny returned quickly. "Oh, Anne, you do understand don't you? I just feel as though I have to get away until some of this hurt and disappointment fades a little."

"Yes, Jenny, I do understand, and David will, too. Shall I write to Aunt Eleanor and suggest you as a secretary-companion, then?"

"Yes, please. And thank you, Anne." Jenny hugged the older woman, grateful for the prospect of an escape, and Anne returned the embrace, glad to be able to help but sorry that it meant Jenny would be leaving.

ELEANOR MACLEAN REPLIED by return mail that she would be more than willing to try Jenny as a secretary-companion, since she had now been without one for more than two weeks and was unable to manage her correspondence alone.

Although written in a rather spidery hand, the letter was brisk and matter-of-fact, recommending that Jenny take the night train to Edinburgh and then come by cab to her house in Charlotte Square. The letter closed with the observation that since space was no problem, then, if she and Jenny still suited one another when the baby was born, the child would be as welcome as his mother.

"And that, my dear," Anne said when she and Jenny had read the letter, "is just what you needed to know. I feel more and more certain that you two will understand each other perfectly." When they handed the letter on to David, he, too, reluctantly agreed with Jenny's decision to go to Edinburgh as soon as possible. The children were harder to convince that Jenny's going was the right thing to do, since she preferred not to explain to them all her reasons for leaving. Finally, though, they accepted her explanation that she wanted to try something new, but would come back to visit them. She delegated the responsibility of her kitchen garden to the twins, and they solemnly promised to take good care of it.

On the day of her departure, the whole family drove her to London. They stopped first at the house in Ennismore Mews, and while the others waited downstairs with Timothy and his wife, Anne went with Jenny up to her beautiful room to collect the rest of her belongings. She was determined to remove every trace of herself, and she packed rapidly in the room that had been hers for such a short time, trying desperately not to remember that last wonderful night with Adam....

When she had finished and David had taken her cases to the car, she hesitated, then walked into Adam's room and placed her lovely engagement ring on the table beside his bed, keeping only the plain wedding band he had given her. For a searing moment she remembered the warmth of his skin, the touch of his hands, the soft rhythm of his breath as he slept beside her, and stifling a sob, she ran from the room.

Downstairs she said goodbye to the kindly Browns, explaining only that she would be staying with friends for a time. She said nothing about Adam's request for a divorce, feeling that when he chose he could find some explanation for them, then shook Timothy's hand and gave his comforting wife a quick, hard hug. Then she left hastily, anxious to go before the observant Mrs. Brown noticed the slight thickening of her waistline and before the images of Adam she saw everywhere became too much to bear.

At King's Cross Station, David found Jenny's train compartment, and the children inspected it thoroughly, fascinated by the idea of her sleeping there most of the way from London to Edinburgh. Then it was time to go.

The twins said goodbye first, Geoffrey looking solemn and Joan sniffing openly. Jenny hugged both of them, then bent and lifted Teddy for a kiss. He smacked his lips against her cheek, then put his finger in his mouth and looked at her in puzzlement, unable to understand what was happening. With a lump in her throat, Jenny handed him back to his father, who said gruffly, "My oldest son is a fool." She kissed his lean cheek and turned to Anne.

For a long moment the two women looked at each other, then Jenny whispered, "Let me know how he is, but don't tell him where I've gone." Anne nodded wordlessly, took both her hands and kissed her. "Thank you," Jenny choked out and hurried into her compartment. Almost immediately the train began to inch from the platform, and soon she was lost from the sight of the small, wildly waving group.

Somewhat to her surprise, Jenny slept soundly in the compact berth as the train pounded northward, its wheels beating out a comforting rhythm. She awoke refreshed and in full command of herself by the time the train pulled into Edinburgh. Jenny disembarked and, after a hot cup of tea and some toast at the railway café, easily found a cab to take her from the station to Anne's great-aunt's in Charlotte Square.

Her driver was a short, sandy-haired man who immediately asked if this was Jenny's first time in Edinburgh; upon learning it was, he took pride in pointing out some of the city's more famous landmarks. He took her part of the way along Princes Street, pointing out the Gothic extravagance of the Scott Monument, the stores so popular with tourists, the Royal Scottish Academy, and Edinburgh Castle massed high above it all. His heavy burr took a minute or two to get used to, but soon she caught the rhythm of his speech and followed his identifications and anecdotes with genuine interest. In the late eighteenth century, the Scottish poet

Robert Fergusson referred vividly to the somewhat odorous Edinburgh of his day as "Auld Reekie," but Jenny found the salt air blowing off the Firth of Forth clear and fresh. While the air in England had a liquid gold quality to it, here, in this cool northern city, it seemed to have a silvery translucency she found invigorating.

Turning toward the Forth they entered Edinburgh's New Town, a monument to town planning with the eighteenth-century elegance of crescents and squares. Charlotte Square proved to be one of the handsomest of these, filled with buildings whose solid, gray stone facades were lightened by beautiful fanlight doorways, delicate stone swags, and graceful, Corinthian half columns.

Jenny's friendly driver located the address and carried her cases up the steps. Jenny rang the bell and the door was opened by an elderly maid whose ruffled apron and starched white cap looked as if they belonged to another century. Faded blue eyes surveyed Jenny dispassionately as she said, "The new secretary? Hope you have more gumption than the last."

Jenny couldn't repress a small chuckle at this blunt greeting, and the other looked more closely at her. "Hmm. Circles under your eyes and cheeks too thin, but you look as though you might have some spirit. Maybe you'll do."

Jenny paid the cab driver and thanked him when he wished her a pleasant stay in the city, then turned back to the small, starched figure at the door to remark, "Maybe I will indeed. I suppose we'll find out soon enough when I meet Mrs. Maclean."

She looked inquiringly at the maid, who shook her head. "She's just getting dressed now. She said I was to show you to your room and give you time to get settled, and then she'd see you downstairs about ten." And with no more ado the crisp white cap turned and led the way across an entrance hall and upstairs, saying over one shoulder, "Don't mind about your cases. I'll have Peter bring them up in a minute."

She showed Jenny into a large white bedroom where big windows and attractive but sparse furnishings gave the room a simple airy look. The only notes of luxury were a bed heaped high with quilts, and a soft flowered carpet, but Jenny immediately felt comfortable in it. After showing her where the bathroom was, the maid—who announced that her name was Agnes and that she'd been with Mrs. Maclean for forty years—left her with a brief word that the cases would be right up.

Nearly an hour later, wearing a soft, gold-plaid wool dress, her makeup freshened and her hair smoothed into a roll at the nape of her neck, Jenny faced her new employer in a beautiful drawing room where pastel green walls provided a background for slender pilasters, light moldings, and graceful ribbons and wreaths of plaster.

Eleanor Maclean, a tiny whitehaired woman in an old-fashioned dress of plum-colored silk, sat regally in a wing chair. One heavily ringed hand rested on the silver knob of a cane, but in spite of that and the white hair, she gave an impression of indomitable vitality. Her skin was surprisingly smooth, and observant green eyes looked shrewdly out on the world; her voice, when it came, was firm. In her youth she must have been a dazzling Edwardian beauty, and in her old age she still retained the confidence—so typical of many beautiful woman—that she could behave exactly as she chose.

This was immediately obvious. Instead of greeting Jenny, she looked her up and down, then barked, "So you're the girl Anne's stepson won't stay married to—and you with a baby on the way. What's he thinking of?"

Momentarily stunned by this frontal attack, Jenny quickly gathered her wits, remembering Anne's description of her great-aunt. "Nothing I'd like to discuss, thank you," she answered matter-of-factly.

There was an instant's silence before the old lady chuckled. "Good girl! It's really none of my business, but when I ask impertinent questions these days people don't usually dare refuse to answer them."

She veered off. "Why did Anne think you'd be suitable for me?"

Jenny paused for a minute, studying the diminutive figure in front of her, then replied calmly, "Because I'm a good secretary and because you won't be able to intimidate me, Mrs. Maclean."

This time Eleanor Maclean laughed openly. "You might as well call me Aunt Eleanor the way Anne does, because I think you're going to be here as long as I can keep you. Now come sit down and tell me where you're from originally and who your people are."

During the next few weeks Jenny settled into life in Charlotte Square and into Aunt Eleanor's routine. They both rose rather late and breakfasted separately, then they met to discuss letters that required answering and arrangements that had to be made for charity benefits and fund drives. The older woman would rest for an hour or two, a habit that Jenny herself soon fell into.

In the afternoons she sometimes accompanied Aunt Eleanor in the venerable limousine, which Peter drove with stately slowness, on errands or visits to friends. At other times she chose to walk by herself, learning her way around the city and delighting in each new piece of history she discovered.

Not surprisingly, one of the first places Jenny explored was the famous and romantic Royal Mile. She began at the upper end, investigating Edinburgh Castle and lingering in the eleventh-century chapel of St. Margaret, the great

Banqueting Hall and the little room where Mary, Queen of Scots, gave birth to the baby who would be James VI of Scotland and James I of England. For a moment Jenny felt a wave of sympathy for the queen who, like herself, was estranged from the father of her child; then she thrust such painful thoughts away and concentrated again on history.

Leaving the castle she walked past St. Giles Church with its crown of stone lace, down the High Street by the home of the fiery church reformer, John Knox, along the Canongate to the great square in front of the Palace of Holyrood, whose quiet stones had seen much of the drama and passion of Scottish history.

During that lonely but tranquil spring, Jenny discovered many places she grew to love, such as quiet Dean Village in the heart of the noisy city, the Rhododendron Walk in the Botanical Gardens, and the ingenious Flower Clock in the gardens along Princes Street. Her love for Adam was with her constantly, but as she strolled in favorite parts of the city her bitterness and grief eased to a sort of gentle longing.

Gradually, though, her walks became shorter, and she went out less often on the afternoon errands and to the evening concerts she had attended with Aunt Eleanor. Instead, as time passed, Jenny found herself becoming too cumbersome to be very active and was content, as summer wore on, to miss most of Edinburgh's famous festival and spend more time in the house in Charlotte Square.

Aunt Eleanor had designated the little room adjacent to Jenny's to be used as the nursery, and Jenny enjoyed preparing it. She bought a length of pretty, lemon-colored material and sewed curtains, then began searching for furniture to put in the room. From Aunt Eleanor's storeroom she borrowed a chest of drawers and a deep, comfortable rocking chair, much like the one that had been a part of her own childhood. On one of her outings she visited the

Lawnmarket, and there, in an antique shop, discovered an old cradle glowing with the patina of age. She fell in love with it at once and took it home triumphantly in a cab. Once Peter had installed it in the sunny nursery, she polished its shining wood until it gleamed more than ever; she loved to touch it, dreaming of other babies whose sleep it had sheltered. She also began to buy clothing and soft linens for the baby, accumulating them in neat piles through which she often sorted simply for the pleasure of handling them.

Aunt Eleanor professed to take no interest in all this, declaring she had no personal use for children until they reached an age when they could talk intelligibly; nevertheless, she often came in to check on Jenny's progress with the little room. Of course, she always explained that she had come only because she knew that that was where she'd find Jenny when she needed her.

Eventually Jenny spent nearly all her free time in the nursery. When she wasn't actually working on it, she often just sat in the rocking chair and dreamed or read or wrote letters.

Her brief notes to Miss Mayfair and Blair Graham said only that she was visiting a friend for a while and asked them to write her in Edinburgh. To Dr. Pennington, however, she wrote in somewhat more detail.

She had answered a letter from him soon after Adam's accident, telling him only how it had happened. His concerned reply came almost immediately, and she was ashamed that she had not answered it before this. Her oldest friend deserved more from her than that. Now she wrote to him, telling him that she and Adam were getting divorced and that she was working in Edinburgh at a job she enjoyed. She found she couldn't tell even Dr. Pennington about the baby, though, fearing that he might be upset to learn that she intended raising the child alone.

She wrote frequently to Repose as well, brightening her letters with anecdotes about Aunt Eleanor and little sketches of her own increasing size, reassuring them that she was well. In return she received an occasional loving scrawl from the twins and regular letters from Anne, full of family news that sometimes also included news of Adam's progress through two operations, each one followed by a long period of convalescence that, David reported, sorely tried his son's disposition.

Reading Anne's letters in the sun-drenched peace of her nursery, Jenny was wrung with love and pity for Adam, knowing well how caged and desperate being an invalid would make him feel. Carrying his child, she understood and loved the father more than ever in the serenity she had finally achieved, and she prayed that the operations would succeed.

But for all her concern, she found that her brief marriage to Adam seemed rather remote as the approaching birth of his child dominated her thoughts, insulating her from everything else. Then one day as she sat at her typewriter she felt a sudden pain. And, on a cold clear November morning, after a few blurred hours of agony, the tiny mewling bundle that was Owen David Standish lay beside her.

CHAPTER FOURTEEN

It wasn't until after the second operation, in early October, that Adam was even able to use a wheelchair, but as soon as he gained that much mobility he was determined to leave the nursing home. Knowing from Anne's last visit that she had insisted on taking Jenny back to Repose, he assumed she was either still there or home in Cornwall and made plans to return to Ennismore Mews.

Timothy and Mrs. Brown had converted the handsome library into a temporary bedroom because Adam refused to install an elevator or let Timothy carry him up and down the stairs. Thus, one Sunday afternoon, Timothy collected his employer at the nursing home and brought him back to the house. He was soon settled in the library, and Timothy lit the fire while Mrs. Brown produced a pot of tea.

As she bustled around the room making sure that Adam was as comfortable as possible, Mrs. Brown said cheerfully, "Well, now, Mr. Standish, I suppose your young wife will be bringing herself and her belongings right home now that you're back."

Adam's fingers clenched the teacup he held, but he said in a cool and controlled voice, "No, I think not, Mrs. Brown. We're going to be divorced."

Mrs. Brown stopped in her tracks. "Oh dear! Why, she never said . . . but you . . ." she murmured in confusion, then looked helplessly at her husband.

Timothy was as shocked as she was, but he simply shook his head at her and glanced toward the door, saying to Adam, "Well, we're very sorry to hear that, sir. If you have everything you need, we'll leave you alone to rest if you like.''

Adam nodded curtly, and the pair went out, leaving him to stare into the fire. He had not been in this room since the night Jenny had come to him there, worried about his cold. He saw again the concern in her eyes, the absurd bare feet and the gleam of silken skin through the flimsy nightgown that had so embarrassed her. And he remembered how her passion had flamed to meet his. He dropped his head into his hands, and Timothy's kind words echoed tauntingly around him, ''If you have everything you need. . . .''

A long time later he wheeled himself over to the telephone and called David at Repose to say that he was safely home and would go in to the publishing offices in the morning; David need not come to town but should take a well-deserved break.

Knowing how his son had chafed at his long inactivity, David made no protests, not even offering to join Adam at the office the first day or two until he was settled in again. He only agreed quietly, and in the morning Adam had Timothy drive him to work in the roomy old Rolls he had owned for years but seldom driven.

With the help of Jenny's capable replacement, Adam was soon caught up with those few details David had forgotten to keep him posted on, and he worked at a ferocious pace the rest of the day. He was well aware that Dr. Llewellyn would have strongly disapproved of his activities, but they gave him an outlet for the energy that otherwise would have turned inward to thoughts he preferred to escape. When Timothy drove him home late that afternoon, he was too exhausted to do more than toy with Mrs. Brown's excellent meal. He went to bed almost immediately after dinner, dropping into the heavy, dreamless sleep he had hoped for.

In the weeks that followed he continued to work at the

same desperate speed. When he reluctantly visited Dr. Llewellyn for one of his periodic examinations, the consultant warned him that he was probably asking too much of himself, but Adam refused to slow down. The doctor might have objected more strenuously to his patient's conduct had he not remembered Jenny and guessed perceptively that Adam needed work as a release from thoughts of the wife he refused to see but seemed to miss. He had no intention of interfering in Adam's private life, however, so he contented himself with a warning. As it happened, Adam finally adjusted to the pace he set himself and grew gradually less tired by it.

When he saw Dr. Llewellyn again, the consultant felt that his health seemed to be stable and that he would soon be fit for the next operation. "I must warn you, though, that because the two earlier operations were not completely successful, this one will be the most delicate of all. I still believe you will walk again, but I cannot guarantee success this time, either; if this operation fails it will be a long time before we can try again."

Adam agreed grimly and made his preparations to return to the hospital. David came to London and spent a day in the company offices with Adam, in preparation for taking over again. That night he stayed with his son in Ennismore Mews and in the morning drove Adam through a rainy December day to the hospital.

On the way Adam broke the silence to say, "I'm sorry to be constantly calling on you to come up here and manage the company again. I meant to take the weight of that off your shoulders after all these years."

"Nonsense," his father returned. "I certainly don't mind having to work occasionally."

Nothing more was said in the car, and soon they reached the hospital. Before David left, Adam looked at the older

man for a long moment, wanting to ask about Jenny; she must
have returned to Cornwall long since, but surely the family
heard from her sometimes—unless she managed to blot out
of her life everything that had to do with him and the few
short weeks of their marriage. He had done nothing more
about the divorce and realized now with a spasm of pain that
as soon as he left the hospital he should take care of the legal
requirements, as it was very likely Jenny would want to
marry again. Neither he nor David had spoken of her,
however, since he'd asked his father to take that letter to her,
and finally he said a muted goodbye without mentioning her.

As Dr. Llewellyn had warned, the operation was long and
difficult, and followed by more weeks of convalescence and
grinding therapy. But when at last David drove his son home
to Ennismore Mews at the beginning of February, Adam was
walking, leaning heavily on a stick that Dr. Llewellyn said
would eventually be unnecessary.

David stayed for dinner, and afterward he and Timothy
helped Adam upstairs to his own room before David said
good night and started back to Repose, leaving Adam to look
musingly around the bedroom he hadn't seen for almost a
year.

A glint of gold caught his eye, and he moved with
difficulty toward the table by his bed. And there lay the
beautiful engagement ring Jenny had put there many months
before and Mrs. Brown had not moved. As he picked it up,
the gems glowed at him, reminding him why he had chosen
that combination—sapphires for the color of Jenny's eyes
and an opal for the subtle, shifting warmth of her personality.
His fingers closed so tightly around the ring that it dug into
his palm, and he moved with awkward speed into Jenny's
lovely aqua and ivory room, even going into her dressing
room to find some trace of her. There was nothing; her room
was as empty of her being as it had been when the decorator

had finished with it, before that wedding night that was no wedding night.

Back in his own room he sank onto the edge of the bed, staring unseeingly at the far wall.

When morning arrived, cast in pale winter sunlight, Adam arose from an almost sleepless night. He pulled on dark slacks and an old tweed jacket and made his way stiffly down the stairs, where after only a few bites of breakfast he announced he was going to the country for the day.

Timothy began to protest, "But, sir, you've only just begun walking again—"

"I'm not walking, I'm driving," Adam interrupted with all the cool mockery at his command. His quelling look silenced even Mrs. Brown, who would otherwise have felt it her duty to discourage such recklessness. With no more than a reproachful look, she packed him a lunch; then she and Timothy saw Adam off in the big Rolls. As the car disappeared from view, they tried to reassure each other that surely a short drive wouldn't hurt him and that, of course, he must be going to Repose.

They were wrong: he was going much farther. Free and mobile for the first time in a year, he drove southwest from London and settled into a steady pace. He was going to Cornwall, irresistibly drawn to St. Just and Jenny. Her engagement ring was in his pocket, but all through the long hours of driving he thought only of seeing her again, not of what he'd say when he did.

It was midafternoon when he reached St. Just, and he drove straight through the village to the old stone house. Pulling up in front of it, he levered himself out of the car and walked to the front door. No one responded to his knock, but the door swung open and he stepped into the kitchen, thinking Jenny must have been out and he might as well wait in the cheerful room he remembered.

His eyes swept it, seeing the beamed ceiling, the old hutch filled with china, the rocking chair he had sat on when he came to take Jenny to Repose for Christmas and their wedding. The room, however, was not entirely the same. On the mantelpiece was propped an unframed portrait of Jenny that had somehow caught her dreaming quality.

Adam stared at it for a long moment, studying the sunlight on the deep brown hair, the clear serenity of the sea blue eyes, the graceful turn of the neck that rose in a smooth, white column from the collar of a faded pink shirt. It was a superb portrait, tender and perceptive, and Adam knew instinctively that it had been painted by someone who loved its subject.

Forcing his eyes away from the portrait, he saw now that a few small landscapes leaned elsewhere in the room, and the smooth, scrubbed table held a scattered sheaf of drawings, many of which were also of Jenny. In addition, he saw a blue bowl of late chrysanthemums on the table and a woman's red jacket hanging by the door.

Adam was nearly in Devon before he slowed the car to a reasonable speed, and then it was because, no longer sustained by his desire to see Jenny, his body was beginning to rebel against the premature demands made on it. Driving became more and more difficult, but he welcomed the labor with bitter desperation: it left him less chance to dwell on the realization that Jenny must be sharing the house with that painter, without even bothering to wait for a divorce.

In the next few hours Adam had to stop several times to rest his aching body, and finally, knowing he hadn't the strength to go all the way back to London, he called the Browns to say he wouldn't be home that night.

"Very good, sir," Timothy responded impassively, but then his concern got the better of him. "You are all right, Mr. Standish?"

"Yes, fine," Adam answered wearily, too aware of the

Browns' kindness to resent the question, "but I'm more tired than I expected, so I shall stay the night at Repose." And with a brief good night, he hung up, leaving Timothy and his wife to assume that they had been right from the start about his destination.

It was very late when he pulled into the long driveway to Repose, and except for a single light upstairs, the house was dark. He let himself in with the key David had always insisted he keep, stumbling slightly at the doorsill and dropping his stick. He swore softly but fluently, and Anne appeared at the top of the stairs, wrapped in an old, plaid dressing gown.

"Adam!" she called softly, and he looked up as she hurried down to him.

She made no comment on the late hour or his haggard appearance and said only, "Come into the lounge, and I'll make you a drink." She handed him the errant stick, and he followed her awkwardly, sinking with relief into a deep leather chair in the little room.

"I'm sorry to come so late, Anne," he appologized with weary good manners. "Did I wake you?"

"No. The children and David are asleep, but I stayed up reading a thriller I finished just as you arrived," she replied, her matter-of-fact tone removing his fear that he imposed. She handed him a drink and bent to light a small fire on the hearth by his chair. When it was going, she took the chair opposite him and sat down, tucking her feet up under her like a child. Still she asked no questions, only waiting in case he chose to speak.

After a couple of restorative gulps, he held his glass out before him, swirling the liquor and watching how its amber depths caught the firelight. He was silent for a long time, and finally, as if the words were wrenched out of him, he said, "I went down to Cornwall."

Anne made no comment, though she looked at him

speculatively, wondering why he had gone and whether or not his need to talk was great enough to break down the old barriers between them. Wisely, she did not attempt to force his confidence, knowing it would be given only if and when something made him forget the longtime antipathy he had felt toward her. She burrowed more comfortably into her chair and maintained a receptive silence, her eyes watching the flames rise and fall on the hearth.

When at length he began to speak, the words came slowly, their tempo increasing as he went on. In a voice edged with misery, he told her how he had gone to Cornwall that morning because he'd felt impelled to see Jenny. He paused, remembering, and Anne asked quietly, "Why now, Adam?"

He took Jenny's engagement ring from his pocket and wordlessly handed it to Anne. As it rested in her palm, she recollected noticing its absence from Jenny's hand when she'd left for Edinburgh. Anne wondered why his finding it had sent him off on that long drive into the West Country the day after he returned home from a serious operation and weeks of difficult convalescence.

He went on speaking to tell her about the house in St. Just, empty but open when he arrived, and the pictures of Jenny he found there. "Besides that magnificent portrait, full of the very essence of her, there were sketches all over the table in the kitchen, sketches of her laughing, dreaming, reading— Jenny in a hundred moods at a hundred different times, and each sketch done with the perceptiveness of love. I knew she had rented out the house to that painter, Blair somebody or other, and for a moment I didn't understand. Then I saw her jacket hanging there and left the love nest as quickly as possible."

His tone had become cynical on the last sentence, and long tapered fingers tightened on the stem of his glass until it snapped with a sudden, sharp little sound. The amber fluid splashed over his hand, and bright blood welled where the crystal had cut.

Anne murmured in concern and started to uncurl from her chair, but he waved her back with the other hand. He knotted his handkerchief around the gash, pointing out sardonically that the alcohol would make an excellent antiseptic. Then he rested the bandaged hand on his knee and continued speaking as if the broken glass had cut some verbal artery and he couldn't staunch the flow.

"I really don't know why I was so surprised, in fact. Divorce is just another of those little legal formalities almost no one bothers about these days, and I wrote her myself that she would be free of me. So why should she wait? After all, my own mother didn't wait, and she hardly had my father's consent! Did he ever tell you about my mother, Anne?"

She answered the sharp question quietly, although they both knew that David would not have talked about his first wife to his second. "He said only that they were divorced and that she died in Italy a few years afterward."

"Drowned in Italy, to be precise," he corrected acridly. "Drowned because she fell out of her current lover's boat. She was too drunk to swim and he was too drunk to rescue her. After embarrassing my father by her conduct at home, she abandoned us both without a glance, flitting from country to country and lover to lover until her death."

He looked into the fire, so that Anne could see only part of his face, a face ravaged by remembered and fresh disillusionments.

"I was only a boy when she left my father, but I was old enough to see him grieve for her and to realize that loving doesn't bring love in return. All our love for her made no difference; she accepted it as her due and then ran away like a spoiled, greedy child looking for more. Still, she offered me an early lesson that I thought I had learned well, and now

Jenny is giving me a refresher course. I should be grateful to them both for their kind concern for my education.''

Anne's low clear voice ended his bitter monologue. ''Jenny isn't in Cornwall; she hasn't been there since the wedding.''

It seemed at first as if he hadn't heard her. He continued to stare into the fire, but then the saturnine expression that had knotted the dark eyebrows slowly evaporated, leaving his face curiously unguarded. He breathed something indistinguishable and turned his head to look at Anne again.

''She isn't still here?''

''No, she left us a few days after David brought home your letter.'' It was with some difficulty that she kept her voice noncommittal.

''She's taken all her belongings from my house—I looked last night. Anne, where else did she have to go?''

''Nowhere,'' she answered coolly, watching his face. It tensed.

''My God, Anne, you didn't just let her disappear into another tired hostel somewhere? I thought you cared about her, and all these months I've told myself that you'd let her leave here only for some place she'd be happy!''

This time Anne's voice warmed into anger. ''Happy? Why should you care if she's happy or not? You didn't think of her happiness when you wrote her that appalling letter!''

''I thought about nothing else,'' he blazed back. ''How happy do you think she would have been tied for life to a cripple? When I wrote that letter, I had no confidence any operation would ever make me more than the battered, useless hulk I was then, unable to work, unable to care for her. She's young and lovable. . . .'' The hard voice cracked a little, then steadied. ''I thought she could start over again and make a life for herself with someone who's whole and could give her everything she deserves. Blair, for example; he's a brilliant painter who will eventually be very successful, and he obviously loves her.''

"Then why were you so bitterly angry when you thought she was with him? Was that the outraged moralist speaking?'' she inquired sweetly.

He ignored her sarcastic tone and answered quietly, "No, that was another man who loves her.''

Satisfied at last, Anne dropped the role of inquisitor. More gently she asked, "Did Jenny know you loved her?''

"I never told her so; I didn't know myself for such a long time. Once, perhaps, she might have guessed.''

"Once, Adam?''

"Not much to build a marriage on, is it?'' His tone was filled with self-contempt.

"But she would have, you know, even on so little. And a woman in love can build a whole palace of happiness out of just a few fragments of hope. Nor would she care whether or not its king was crippled.''

He looked at her in mingled wonder and disbelief. "My mother would have.''

"Perhaps your mother was unable to love anyone but herself, for all her trying, and that, too, is a kind of crippling, more pathetic than others. But why must you judge all women by one who hurt you?''

"I've judged you by that standard for years.''

"Yes, I know,'' she answered matter-of-factly. "Fortunately, your father has more discrimination.''

"Anne, I'm sorry,'' he said with difficulty. "Can you forgive me for the years I've willfully cast you in my mother's mold and tried to divide my father's loyalties?''

"Of course,'' she said simply.

A long look that carried respect and understanding passed between them; then Adam dropped his eyes to the bandaged hand lying in his lap, and slowly his face slipped back into its unhappy lines.

For a while the only sound was the crackling of the fire. Finally Anne spoke softly. ''What will you do now, Adam?''

He struggled to his feet and moved stiffly across the room to stand at one of the long windows, pulling back the curtain so he could look out into the darkened garden where once, in a spring that seemed very long ago, he had found Jenny lying sleepy and tumbled under a loving heap of children.

Without turning back to Anne, he answered wearily, ''I don't really know, except that I have to find Jenny. I'll check with Miss Mayfair to see if she's heard from her, and I can go back to Cornwall, I suppose, and see both Dr. Pennington and the painter. If he isn't just paying rent into a bank account, Blair may have an address for her. I don't know of any other friends she might have turned to after she left here.''

Anne recognized his assumption that, since she had volunteered no information, she knew nothing about Jenny's whereabouts, but for the moment she decided to let the assumption stand.

Adam continued to speak in the same tone that was a blend of exhaustion and determination. ''My lawyer has no address for her since she left the mews, and when I thought she was home in Cornwall or here with you I didn't worry too much about her allowance. If she's on her own, though, she may be in need of money.''

''And if she isn't?''

''Then I suppose there's nothing else I can give her,'' he said flatly.

''The only thing she ever wanted was your love.''

''She has it and always will, but it's a bit late to be offering her my heart when she's expecting a divorce instead.''

''Have you completed the legal arrangements?''

"No," he admitted, "I've done nothing more about them at all. I suppose I should take care of them so she can be free of the whole tragic mess of our marriage."

"Why don't you ask her if she wants to be free?" Anne suggested softly.

Her voice had a low note of something that might have been humor, and as he caught the sound of it, Adam let the curtain drop down in front of the window and slowly turned to look at her. His body was tense and his lean face completely still.

"How?" he asked hoarsely.

"Go to Charlotte Square in Edinburgh and ask my Great-Aunt Eleanor if you may speak to her secretary-companion," she answered, then added in laughing protest, "Adam, not now! It's the middle of the night!"

Moving with astonishing speed, he crossed the room to give Anne a brief hard squeeze and headed toward the door, saying briskly over his shoulder, "Yes now! So I can be there by morning!"

"Adam, no." She unwound from her chair, disentangling her feet from the old dressing gown, and caught him at the door. "You can't talk to Jenny if you're too tired to be coherent. You have to have some rest first if you're going to be able to manage that long drive—especially after everything you've been through today. In fact, if you had any sense at all you'd go by train."

"We agreed earlier that I haven't shown much sense," he reminded her with the ghost of his old mocking smile, but reluctantly he let himself be persuaded into going upstairs for a few hours' sleep.

Adam found the trip up the long flight of stairs difficult. He used his left hand to haul himself up, and Anne slipped her shoulder under his on the right, replacing his stick. When they finally reached the top of the staircase, they were both breathing heavily, but Adam managed to say, "We all lean on you, don't we?"

Anne blushed a little and said breathlessly, "The only extra bed I have made up is Jenny's, Adam, so you'll have to sleep there."

He looked at her a moment and then said with a mixture of wistful longing and dry humor that made her smile, "It'll be a pleasure."

When they reached Jenny's room, Adam sank thankfully onto the edge of the bed while Anne gave him directions to her Aunt Eleanor's. Then she murmured a good night and turned to go; at the door she looked back and asked, "Shall I call the Browns tomorrow and ask David to see to things in London for a while?"

Adam answered slowly. "Yes, please. Whatever happens in Edinburgh, I don't think I'll be back right away."

She nodded. "I'll put a few things of David's in a suitcase for you and leave it at the door, in case you're on your way before I wake up in the morning. But do get some sleep first," she added, daring to sound like the mother he'd never really had.

Her tone elicited a beautiful and rather rare smile from Adam, and as she went out he called softly, "Anne . . . thank you."

She shut the door of Jenny's room behind her and, alone in the hallway, wandered its length for some time, questioning her decision to tell Adam where Jenny had gone without telling him she was there with his son. She worried about her sins of commission and omission but finally gave it up and went to search through David's wardrobe with quiet fingers, finding things his son could wear.

When the small suitcase she located was packed with a few essentials, she left it outside the door of Jenny's room where Adam—she hoped—was sleeping by now. That done, she slipped away to her own bed and crept in without disturbing David.

When she arose in the morning, Adam was gone, and she told only his father about his brief visit.

CHAPTER FIFTEEN

FOR ADAM the long miles northward unrolled slowly, a black ribbon of impatience stretching endlessly in front of him. Thanks to Anne, the previous day's determination to see Jenny was stronger than ever, and as the morning wore on, he drove the Rolls with abstracted skill through the Midlands and on to the quieter border country.

It was just before noon when he drove into Charlotte Square and found the number Anne had given him. He pulled up and eased himself from the car, reaching behind for his stick. He thought wryly—and a bit nervously—that he'd prefer not to look any more decrepit than necessary, but balancing precariously on unsteady legs he knew his only choices were use the stick or risk a fall. He chose the former. Moving cumbersomely between iron railings whose sharp-pointed tips made him a little uneasy, he climbed the five stone steps to the fanlight doorway that had received Jenny the previous spring.

At his knock, Agnes opened the door. She looked him up and down and barked a curt ''Yes?''

Adam simply stared at her for a moment, slowly realizing that he had unconsciously expected Jenny to open the door as if she were the only person in the house. At last he pulled himself together and said, ''May I see Mrs. Standish, please? I'm Adam Standish.''

The faded blue eyes peered at him more intently, and then Agnes said ''Hmmph!'' in a way that was not encouraging—nor was it, in fact, meant to be. She seemed undecided for a minute but finally snapped, "Well, I'll take you to Mrs. Maclean."

This was certainly not the purpose of his trip, but Adam reasoned it would at least get him off the doorstep and inside the house, so he nodded and followed her in. At the drawing-room door she announced, "This is that Standish man, come to see Jenny." Then she wheeled and left, disapproval in every starched line of her. Adam stared at the regal little figure the maid had addressed.

Eleanor Maclean sat in the same wing chair that Jenny had first found her in, and the months since then had not in the least diminished her autocratic vitality.

"Well, don't just stand there, young man. Come in and sit down before you fall down."

One of his mobile black eyebrows rose at the barked command, but admitting the truth of her shrewd observation, Adam stiffly crossed the room and took the chair she indicated with an imperious hand.

From the front of a sea green, watered-silk dress of ageless style, she lifted a lorgnette and peered at him through it, an affectation that amused her. She studied him for a disconcertingly long time, but Adam forced himself to remain still throughout the scrutiny. Satisfied at last, she let the lorgnette fall and spoke abruptly. "So why should I let you see Jennifer?"

Anne had not taken the time the previous night to give Adam the briefing on her aunt's ways that she had given Jenny, so he was not prepared for these sudden verbal attacks. Nevertheless, he met her opening shot with one of his own.

"Since she's my wife, you can't very well refuse to let me see her."

"Oh ho, can I not in my own house? I could have you put out immediately," she countered.

"Then I would sit on your doorstep and make a public nuisance of myself, embarrassing you and probably necessitating a visit from the police to remove me from the premises," he responded smoothly, eyes glinting.

She gave a tiny snort and shifted her ground. "You've come to visit your wife, have you? I thought there was a little matter of a divorce."

"Jennifer is still my wife," Adam answered flatly.

Eleanor Maclean eyed him for a moment, then inquired mildly, "How did you know she was here?"

"Anne told me."

"When?"

"Late last night."

"And you're here this noon; I think you've been speeding, young man. What else did Anne tell you?"

"Only that Jenny was your secretary-companion."

"One that I should hate to lose. Shall I?"

For the first time in their verbal duel, he looked away from her, saying slowly, "I don't know. I hope so, but that depends entirely on Jenny. May I see her?"

The old woman looked at him, her green eyes sparkling from the rapid give-and-take of their conversation. Like his delightful wife this young man with the arrogant eyebrows and exhausted face was not to be intimidated by an overbearing old lady, and she was amused by her failure. With one beringed hand she made a gesture that might have been a fencer's salute to a worthy opponent and said graciously, "Of course you may. At present I believe Jennifer is in the library, across that little anteroom. I'll let you show yourself in."

He sketched a ghost of a bow to the fascinating and imperious little figure before him, then turned and walked slowly away in the direction indicated. She watched him with an expression of mingled amusement, compassion and regret.

On the far side of the anteroom, the library door swung open at Adam's touch to reveal another high-ceilinged room graced with delicate plaster embellishments on nearly every surface. Its cool elegance was warmed by the rich colors of the books lining the walls and by the fire burning on the hearth. Near the fireplace, at a desk whose graceful lines were countered by the utilitarian machine on its top, Jenny sat typing. She worked with the neat precision Adam remembered, and her body was turned so that he could see only the soft line of her cheek and a few tiny wisps of hair below the smooth roll at the back of her head.

Blindly drawn to her, he moved awkwardly into the room. He was halfway across the thick rug when his stick landed on something flat that immediately skated away. The stick fell with a muffled sound, and when he had regained his balance Jenny was on her feet staring at him, her blue eyes wide with shock and her face the same shade as the ivory sweater she wore.

For a short eternity they simply stared at each other, both incapable of speech or further motion. Finally Adam croaked in a parody of a voice, "Oh God, Guinevere, how can I throw myself at your feet and ask for forgiveness when I've dropped the wretched stick and can't *get* to your feet?"

Laughter and tears struggling on her face, she crossed the room to him and picked up the stick, handing it to him wordlessly. With a broken chuckle, he used it to lower himself to his knees; then gray eyes, their color deepened with emotion, looked up at her as he searched for words.

"Jenny," he began haltingly, "can you forgive me for being too haunted by my own past to dare believe you loved me or admit I loved you?"

She made a tiny, choked sound and dropped swiftly to her knees beside him. While the stick fell again, this time unnoticed, her shaking hands reached to cradle him against her. Their breathing was ragged when he whispered, "I thought that I could learn to live without you and that you'd be better off without me."

Any answer she might have made was lost in his kiss. They clung to each other, passion tempered by wonder, murmuring occasionally and unaware of time and space until the library door opened and a dry voice spoke.

"Am I to assume, Jennifer, that I'm about to lose another secretary?"

Completely unabashed at being found kneeling on the rug with his wife in his arms, Adam reached for his stick and struggled to his feet, but Jenny, scarlet faced, leaped to hers.

Suddenly aware she'd been asked a rather meaningful question, Jenny stammered "Yes . . . oh no . . . I haven't . . . ." With a sudden, cold shock she realized that Adam had said nothing about the baby. The wild-rose color in her cheeks faded slowly, leaving them pinched and whiter than before.

Watching her, Adam seemed almost to age as the tender, triumphant light in his own face died out. He bowed slightly in Aunt Eleanor's direction and said flatly, "Until I can persuade my wife to risk her heart with me again, it appears I may yet have to sit on your doorstep."

"Nonsense, young man. There's an excellent hotel in the Square," the old lady retorted, while her shrewd eyes assessed the two who stood before her. In the set lines of Adam's tired face she read a stubborn determination not to lose Jenny again; from Jenny's tormented eyes she guessed the cause of the girl's hesitation.

For a moment they formed a tableau, then the old woman spoke decisively. "Mr. Standish, I shall expect you here for dinner at seven. In the meantime, I suggest you get a room at the hotel and find some of the sleep you appear to have lost, while Jennifer has a chance to collect her wits."

Her tone was commanding, but Adam met her eyes and recognized both wisdom and sympathy there. He nodded a brief agreement, then turned to Jenny, standing motionless beside him, and brushed her forehead with a kiss. At the door he murmured a goodbye to Aunt Eleanor and was gone.

As the door clicked behind him, Jenny covered her face with her hands.

"You've never told him about the baby, have you?" The question came in a voice gentler than Jenny had heard Aunt Eleanor use before, and in response she shook her head.

In a muffled voice she said, "I never did, and I made the family promise not to, either. I was about to tell him when he wrote me asking for a divorce."

"Why did you change your mind?"

Jenny dropped her hands and exclaimed, "Because I didn't want a man who was a husband only because he was a father!"

"Well, then Jennifer," the other replied, her tone brisk again, "I don't see any problem. That very determined man wants to be a husband without even *knowing* he's a father."

"But now he'd have to be both! Oh, Aunt Eleanor, how can I tell him he has found a wife and baby when all he came looking for was a wife?"

Jenny was too distressed to recognize the contradiction in her words. Aunt Eleanor put up her lorgnette and calmly surveyed Jenny's face. "There, my dear," she said with a touch of humor, "you will have to find your own way with that man, and I shall leave you to do so immediately after dinner this evening."

And with that, the upright little figure turned and walked regally out of the room.

Alone again in the quiet library, Jenny wandered back to her desk and stood at it, gazing unseeingly at the half-finished letter in her typewriter. She didn't sit down to it, though, but paused irresolutely, wondering wretchedly what his reaction to their child would be.

Yet, at the same time, singing through her being was a great joy at the sight of Adam, thinner and more drawn perhaps, but able to walk. At his first words and the touch of his lips and hands, joy had drowned out all else, and she had responded instinctively with all the love she'd been forced to stifle for so long. And the tenderness and awe of his own response had reaffirmed everything they'd both felt that one enchanted winter night.

Absentmindedly, Jenny shredded a letter she had finished just before Adam came in, and her thoughts churned on. If she returned to Adam, she would be giving him not only a wife who adored him but also a child whose existence would be an unexpected and perhaps unwelcome surprise. Their time together had been so short, and their time as man and wife shorter still; Adam might well be reluctant to have his family increased to three so soon.

A log crumbling on the hearth ended Jenny's abstraction, and she walked to the fire to poke the embers safely back into the fireplace. Straightening again, she looked around the beautiful room as if it could somehow resolve her dilemma. Soon she became conscious of the time, realizing that the baby would probably be awake and demanding imperiously to be fed.

She hurried out of the library and upstairs to the sunny nursery, where her son had just decided to exercise his lungs. At the sight of her, he thought better of it and gave her a crooked, toothless grimace that she chose to take for a smile. She leaned over the side of his cradle to watch tiny starfish hands and miniature feet wave. Enthralled by her son, Jenny abandoned the search for a solution to her problem for the time being.

WITH A SORT OF GRIM PATIENCE Adam moved the now dusty
Rolls to the front of the excellent hotel in the Square and
registered, taking in with him the case of David's clothes. His
room was comfortable, and he took some time to wash away
the long hours of travel. His aching body, driven for a day
and a half by the urgent demands made on it, craved sleep. He
stretched his lean length on the bed, hoping sleep would
come, but his churning mind prevented it. Over and over he
tried to figure out Jenny's behavior.

She had met his kisses with a warmth and passion he'd had
no right to expect, setting his senses on fire and dispersing the
last vestige of distrust that had been his mother's bitter
legacy. Then suddenly she had withdrawn from him into
some far place he couldn't follow, and uncomprehending, he
had known only that he couldn't let her go. He had driven her
away once; if she fled from him now, she would take with her
everything in his life that was meaningful.

Tired but restless, Adam got up again and moved to stand
by the window, thinking about Eleanor Maclean's dinner
invitation. He would see Jenny that evening, and he'd see her
again and again if necessary, until he broke down the barriers
she had put up against him. Whatever doubts she had, he'd
overcome them; whatever hesitations, he'd end. He had been
a fool with his happiness once before and would not do so
again.

As sleep was proving impossible as a way to pass the time
until he could be with Jenny again, Adam abandoned his
room and went downstairs. In the hotel dining room, he ate a
quick meal that, for all the attention he gave it, might have
been cold porridge; then, still unable to relax, he walked out
into Charlotte Square. Lost in thought, he paid its gracious
architecture only a perfuntory homage and eventually found
that his uneven steps had taken him to Jenny's front door.

For a moment he simply looked at it, and one eyebrow

went up as he recognized wryly that his longing for Jenny had brought him here without conscious direction. Then on a sudden decision he climbed the steps and knocked; he would not wait until evening to see her again.

When Agnes opened the door, he gave her his most charming smile. "Good afternoon. I would like to see my wife, please."

Prepared to snap as usual, Agnes found herself unaccountably mellowing. Her faded blue eyes blinked uncertainly, and she said doubtfully, "Well, she's in the library typing some letters she didn't finish this morning."

Adam blandly used the smile again. "Thank you. I know the way," and he was past Agnes before she could object.

JENNY HAD NOT ENJOYED her lunch any more than Adam had his. As soon as she left Owen, her doubts and fears caught up with her again. Over lunch she managed only vague and disjointed contributions to Aunt Eleanor's unruffled flow of conversation on every subject except Adam.

The meal finished at last, Aunt Eleanor announced that she was going upstairs. "I think I may rest a bit longer than usual, Jennifer, after this morning's events," she said, then accepted the girl's absentminded agreement. Her shrewd old eyes studied Jenny briefly, but she left the room in her usual dignified way without making any further comment. On her face, however, was a little smile of anticipation that Jenny didn't see and wouldn't have understood if she had seen it. Aunt Eleanor, perhaps, knew the sort of man Adam was better than Jenny did.

Left to her own devices, Jenny found she had absolutely no inclination for a nap and decided to finish the letter Adam's arrival had interrupted; first, though, she wanted to check on the baby. In the nursery she was again so enchanted by her little son that she scooped him out of his cradle, blanket and all, and carried him downstairs with her.

In the library she spread his blanket over the soft rug at a safe but warming distance from the fire and settled Owen onto it. She played delightedly with him for a little while, then sat down at her typewriter. As she worked, she stopped every few minutes to admire the miniature person gurgling on the rug. Jenny experienced a sort of peace in the tranquil room, with her child's chuckles as an accompaniment to the familiar job.

When the letters were done, she left the desk and fetched from across the room—where Adam's stick had sent it flying—a flat, red pull-toy. Then she lay down on the rug with the baby and dragged it back and forth in front of him, laughing tenderly at his joyous burbling.

Entering the room unheard, Adam at first saw only Jenny, sprawled on the rug, and he moved across to her, calling her name in a voice sharpened with worry.

Startled, she swung toward him and sat up; her movement revealed the baby, and Adam stared at his son.

Unlike the tiny copy in front of him, Adam's face was totally still, and watching it anxiously, Jenny felt sick with dismay. Then he walked over to her side and carefully lowered himself to the rug. Without looking at her now, he spoke her name in an unrecognizable voice. "Jenny?"

Her own voice, barely a thread of sound, answered the question he hadn't been able to ask. "Your son, Adam," she said, and searched his face for his reactions.

For a long time Adam looked into the small face near his own, seeing the wisps of dark hair and the miniature winged eyebrows over eyes that were still infant blue. Attracted to this new person, the baby waved a hand in his direction. Adam reached out the tip of one long finger, and the tiny hand clung to it.

It might have been one minute or ten before he turned to face Jenny, and when he did she steeled herself.

Instead of the surprise and irritation she half expected, she found a crooked smile and tears on Adam's angular cheeks. While she was still gazing at him in wonder and disbelief and hope, he said in a cracked voice, "Like a white wave of joy, Jenny."

She looked into his clear gray eyes, where the flame leaped once again, and with a stifled cry she threw herself into his arms. They closed around her, as her lips met his in a kiss that tasted of salt tears. And for a long time small Owen kicked and chuckled, unnoticed by his parents.

HARLEQUIN CLASSIC LIBRARY

Great old romance classics from our early publishing lists.

FREE BONUS BOOK

On the following page is a coupon with which you may order any or all of these titles. If you order all nine, you will receive a FREE book—*Doctor Bill*, a heartwarming classic romance by Lucy Agnes Hancock.

The thirteenth set
of nine novels in the
HARLEQUIN CLASSIC LIBRARY

Great old favorites...
Harlequin Classic Library

Complete and mail this coupon today!

FREE
BONUS
BOOK

Harlequin Reader Service

In U.S.A.
1440 South Priest Drive
Tempe, AZ 85281

In Canada
649 Ontario Street
Stratford, Ontario N5A 6W2

Please send me the following novels from the Harlequin Classic Library. I am enclosing my check or money order for $1.50 for each novel ordered, plus 75¢ to cover postage and handling. If I order all nine titles at one time, I will receive a FREE book, *Doctor Bill*, by Lucy Agnes Hancock.

☐ 109   ☐ 112   ☐ 115
☐ 110   ☐ 113   ☐ 116
☐ 111   ☐ 114   ☐ 117

Number of novels checked @ $1.50 each =	$_____
N.Y. and Ariz. residents add appropriate sales tax	$_____
Postage and handling	$_____.75
TOTAL	$_____

I enclose _____
(Please send check or money order. We cannot be responsible for cash sent through the mail.)
Prices subject to change without notice.

Name _____
(Please Print)

Address _____
(Apt. no.)

City _____

State/Prov. _____

Zip/Postal Code _____

Offer expires October 31, 1983

30456000000